Ephemeral Wings

Eva Silverfine

Illustrated by Taina Litwak

Black Rose Writing | Texas

The author grants the final approval for this literary material.

First printing

ISBN: 978-1-68513-041-1
PUBLISHED BY BLACK ROSE WRITING
www.blackrosewriting.com

Printed in the United States of America
Suggested Retail Price (SRP) $19.95

Ephemeral Wings is printed in Garamond Premier Pro
Cover and illustrations © Taina Litwak 2022

To Brooklyn, my first rock

Soliloquy of a Venerable Ephemera Who Had Lived
Four Hundred and Twenty Minutes

"It was," said he, "the opinion of learned philosophers of our race, who lived and flourished long before my time, that this vast world could not itself subsist more than eighteen hours; and I think there was some foundation for that opinion, since, by the apparent motion of the great luminary that gives life to all nature, and which in my time has evidently declined considerably toward the ocean at the end of our earth, it must then finish its course, be extinguished in the waters that surround us, and leave the world in cold and darkness, necessarily producing universal death and destruction. I have lived seven of those hours, a great age, being no less than four hundred and twenty minutes long. How very few of us continue so long! By the course of nature, though still in health, I cannot expect to live above seven or eight minutes longer. What now avails all my toil and labor! What the political struggles I have engaged in, for the good of my compatriot inhabitants of this bush, or my philosophical studies for the benefit of our race in general! For, in politics, what can laws do without morals! Our present race of ephemerae will in a course of minutes become corrupt, like those of other and older bushes, and consequently be as wretched. And in philosophy how small our progress! Alas! art is long and life is short! My friends would comfort me with the idea of a name, they say, I shall leave behind me; and they tell me I have lived long enough to nature and to glory. But what will fame be to an ephemerae who no longer exists? And what will become of all history in the eighteenth hour, when the world itself shall come to its end, and be buried in universal ruin?

"To me, after all my eager pursuits, no solid pleasures now remain, but the reflection of a long life spent in meaning well, the sensible conversation of a few good lady ephemerae, and now and then a kind smile and a tune from the ever amiable Brillante."

–Benjamin Franklin

Ephemeral Wings

CHAPTER ONE

DRIFTLESS

Maggie touched down. Her claws grabbed the moss mat, and she pulled her body to the rock. Motionless, she scoured the stream's waters above her for shadows and tasted the waters around her for scent. It seemed safe. How good to be on solid rock again. She waved her gills in a deep breath of relief.

Maggie was a mayfly nymph. Small, transparent, oval gills dressed the sides of her abdomen, and three thin tail filaments stretched out far behind her. Her rich brown skin was hard, and her streamlined body quite compact. She stood on thin legs, but the large, dark wing pads that rose from her back added their weight to her appearance. Maggie's face was long and narrow, with big black eyes and long antennae.

Maggie had landed in swift waters. Even if she weren't set adrift again, she certainly wouldn't find food or shelter here. But downstream always promised better waters, and at least now she had her claws on firm ground. Anxious to reach the end of the rapids before night light appeared, Maggie hurried across the moss mat and onto a broad, mossless plateau. The waters propelled her forward.

Scurrying along so, Maggie stepped right on a porous sponge.

"Oh, excuse me—I'm so sorry—I didn't see you," Maggie apologized with embarrassment as she took a few steps back from the amorphous green and brown streamling. The sponge clung so low to the ground that Maggie had to lift up her tail to bring her eyes to the sponge's height. What the sponge lacked in height, though, she compensated for in length: her pithy body stretched over the rock and out of Maggie's sight.

"No harm done," the sponge excused her. "It's certainly not the first time. Where are you headed in such a hurry?"

Maggie wasn't quite sure which part of the sponge to address. Although appearing to be somewhat rock, somewhat plant, the sponge was, like Maggie, an animal. Her skin wasn't smooth and hard like Maggie's, though, but bumpy, pitted, and full of fine spines. The bumps were her outpores, the pits her inpores, and the spines part of the scaffolding that held her together. Yes, she was an animal, but one very different from Maggie: no eyes, no antennae, no legs. With such a lack of definition, from where did her voice come?

"Downstream," Maggie responded to a cluster of inpores, "to the next pool."

"Oh, you're quite close to the end of fast waters," the sponge said. Her gentle voice seemed to emanate from all her pores.

"Many fish there?" Maggie inquired of the sponge at large.

"I would imagine so. You certainly should wait for dark to cross."

"Oh, certainly," Maggie agreed. She glanced around at what seemed a rather stark plain.

"What's your name?" the sponge asked.

"Maggie. And yours?"

"Teresa," the sponge said. "Where are you coming from?"

"From a pool several riffles upstream." Maggie hesitated but then continued. "I was caught in the drift. Just after my last molt some current in my pool changed," she explained, "and every day I was eating more and more sediment, less and less forage. Everywhere I went the ground was covered with silt. So, I had no choice. I had to leave. The drift seemed the only way to escape, so I let go—but then I couldn't get out of it."

"I remember the drift," Teresa recalled her early childhood; "being lifted from the ground into running waters, trying to swim but instead being carried. I didn't know where the waters would take me, if they would bring me to a hospitable rock. ... But you can travel on by claw now. I take it you're headed to a reach without sediment," Teresa said with a note of amusement in her voice.

"Oh, yes," Maggie replied, taking Teresa quite seriously. "I intend to find some better feeding grounds." Then, thinking of the sponge who had lived on this one rock since infancy, Maggie asked, "What do you do when the waters fill with sediment?"

"Sometimes the waters run poorly, and I must close my pores, but those times pass, and soon the waters are steady and full again."

"But don't you worry that the waters will get worse and worse until ..."

"I can only trust that the waters will get better," Teresa responded. "Anyway, when the waters run poor, aren't they the same throughout the stream?"

Maggie looked at the porous streamling who accepted the waters in their richness and poorness as they arrived at her perch. She didn't have the luxury of looking for new feeding grounds. And without legs, the sponge seemed not to have the restlessness that drove Maggie seeking. But Maggie by nature could not remain settled while her home filled with sediment. She would not grow, feeding on such silt.

Rays of the waning daylight cast Maggie's shadow across the sponge.

"I should be going," Maggie said. "It was very nice meeting you."

"Good bye," Teresa said, "and good luck."

Maggie moved quickly over the streambed. At first the current assisted her advance, but then the strengthening flow began to push her from side to side. She stopped. She was at the base of a mountain that passed into the world of air; she had to find some other route.

Maggie turned upstream but couldn't force her way against the oncoming waters—she would have to go around the mountain. The waters pressed her flat against the stone surface, so her progress was slow. Finally, reaching the side slope of the mountain, she turned parallel to the current. The waters rushed over her, surging through a narrow chasm formed by two peaks. Maggie clung to the rock, lifting each leg slowly, moving it forward only slightly. She tried to stay in the thin layer of water that barely moved at the rock's surface. "Not again in the drift!" she said to herself as if a chant to assist her attempt. "Not again in the drift at the top of a pool!" She neared the mountain's downstream face. The waters broke into wild eddies, whirlpools that could pull her to the depth of the stream. Currents tried to unhinge her claws, tried to pry her from the rock by her tail. She clasped the wrinkles of the mountain's face and, hugging its surface, moving slowly, she finally reached the quiet waters in the lee of the stone.

Maggie was just above the pool now. Slender filaments of *cladophora* wafted in the current from the mountain behind her. She waved her gills rhythmically in relief. Only those streamlings who could remain well anchored could manage the erosive currents of the rapids.

Maggie wasn't alone: a large group of swollen-bottomed black flies congregated on nearby rocks, as did some flat-bodied sideswimmers. She saw in the distance a few other mayflies. Waiting with these other itinerants for dark, Maggie found herself thinking of the great flood many molts ago, the flood that had taken her from her first home. She hadn't wanted to leave that pool. There she felt secure among seemingly stable rocks rich with forage. But then the great flood had come, and boulders had tumbled, and she had been washed adrift.

Since then, Maggie had been in the drift a few times, and although she had always managed to find her way to solid ground again, she had learned that she had little control over the particular circumstances to which she arrived.

It was dark now. More travelers had arrived, and some had begun to move into the pool. Night light would soon appear. Maggie headed forward.

Maggie found herself entering the pool on a gentle slope. There were fish here. Maggie couldn't see them, but she could feel their erratic movements. They were waiting at the top of the pool to prey upon those poor unfortunates who hadn't been able to get out of the drift in fast waters. Those on claw weren't completely safe either, but at least they were less conspicuous. Maggie moved through the top of the pool quickly, but she wasn't hasty. Movement was the surest thing a fish would notice.

The current became slower and more steady, fanning out over gentle slopes that were covered with fine fields of algae. Once well beyond the top of the pool, Maggie foraged through the early night light. She then found a crevice just wide enough for a mayfly, and within the safety of the cranny, she went to sleep. It had been a long day.

CHAPTER TWO

GRAIN DISTINCTIONS

"Wow! Look at this!"

Maggie stopped eating and looked around. In the first rays of daylight, down slope from where she stood, she saw a shiny yellow head bent downward. Assuming that she was being addressed, Maggie approached the fly larva expectantly. "What is it?" she asked.

The midge looked up, extended his stubby forelegs forward, and said, "A perfect trapezohedron of cinnabar!" Then, realizing Maggie was unenlightened, he added, "Quite rare, quite rare."

Maggie peered forward and searched amongst the bristles of his setaceous mitts to find the treasure.

"Oh, I see," she said, looking at a bright red stone. "It's, uhm, quite nice. ... What did you call it?"

"Cinnabar. A perfect prismatic cleavage," he said and then stopped as if to catch his breath. "Could mistake it for realgar. But realgar is more orange in color, more resinous in luster. And, of course, realgar is monoclinic—only one axis of twofold symmetry. Oh," he stopped abruptly, "you're probably not familiar with your axes of symmetry."

Actually, Maggie hadn't followed most of what the midge had said. Instead, she had watched his stubby hindlegs, which wandered with each of his statements, continuously changing the orientation of his tubular body, as if the midge were about to set off in a new direction.

"See here. Cinnabar has three axes of twofold symmetry." He held the six-sided crystal by a pair of its opposing faces and showed it to Maggie. Then the midge flipped the grain over, and the faceted face that appeared was identical to the one that had just disappeared. He shifted the crystal in his mitts and rotated it again, revealing the second axis of twofold symmetry. "Realgar, being monoclinic, has only one axis— but you don't know what realgar is, do you?"

"No," Maggie responded with a shake of her head. She looked at the grain he held; it looked somewhat like a dragonfly's head.

"My collection is just over in the shallows," the midge said and started off purposefully.

Maggie took this to be an invitation, so in two steps she was beside him. He was a long fly, and, for having only two pairs of short legs, he moved quite fast. Even so, Maggie had to slow her pace considerably so as not to race ahead of him.

"You're of the Baetidae family, aren't you?" he asked.

"Yes."

"A member of the Centroptilum clan?"

"Yes," Maggie confirmed again. She was a bit surprised; she'd never met a midge before who so readily recognized her clan.

"And you?" she asked politely.

"Chironomidae, Rheotanytarsus." He lifted his face, quickly peeked at Maggie's large eyes, and then added, "Name, Rensaleer. And you?"

"Maggie."

"Baetidae are good swimmers," Rensaleer stated. "Prefer a rock terrain, a moderately swift current, and a diet of algae, correct?"

"Yes," Maggie responded, somewhat confused as to why Rensaleer was listing the habits of her family.

"You undergo several molts," Rensaleer continued, "increasing in size but not changing much in form. That is, until you molt into your adult form. Correct?"

"Yes—"

"Thought I recognized you," Rensaleer said with another quick peek at Maggie's face.

Rensaleer's eyes were small black disks, two on each side of his face, a slightly larger one just above a smaller one. Between his eyes, mounted in the middle of his forehead on conspicuous prominences, was a pair of long, thick-based antennae that arched out in front of him somewhat askew. His wide mouth sat below his antennae. A round-toothed lower lip met an indistinct upper one, and from between them protruded a pair of large, triangular crushing jaws, or mandibles. His head was pale yellow, squarish, and very smooth except for some minute hairs.

With his hard, shiny head went a soft, cylindrical, olive-green body. He was as long as Maggie plus half her length again. His body was carried by two pairs of stubby legs with bristly palms; one pair was situated close to Rensaleer's head, and the second was at the other end of his otherwise undifferentiated body. A tuft of stiff bristles rode on his rump.

"Ah, here we are," Rensaleer announced.

Rensaleer did indeed live in the shallows. The waters barely moved, and the flat terrain on which they stood was covered with sediment. Maggie created a dust cloud as she undulated her gills in a flurry for air. Rensaleer pointed with his antennae to his lodgings.

Barely distinguishable from the sediment in which it was built was Rensaleer's home. It looked like some unexplained accumulation of plant fragments, sand grains, and pieces of unidentifiable origins. On closer inspection, Maggie could see that Rensaleer had constructed a silken tent not much longer than himself and had cemented the aforementioned fragments to it, although some pieces had come to rest there on their own. The tent was conical, and at its wide, upstream entrance, a net ladened with leaf fragments, algae, twigs, grit, and floc bulged inward. The net strained Rensaleer's food from the water.

Although his food net was quite overburdened and needed attention, Rensaleer was anxious to tend to his latest find. Maggie followed him across the flat basin and around a tall, rounded hill at its far border. On the other side of the hill, they climbed down onto a broad ledge.

The slow, silty waters of the shallows disoriented Maggie. Upstream didn't seem to be in any particular direction— actually it felt as if there were no direction at all. But when Maggie eventually did turn to face upstream, she saw a dazzling structure.

"What is this?" she asked, but Rensaleer was already far ahead. She took a few steps forward.

Rensaleer had used his building skills to construct a mesh wall that stretched from the back side of the rounded hill, across the ledge on which they stood, and downward to where it attached to another flat rock surface. At most of the junctures of this silk lattice were cemented grains. These grains were of all sizes, shapes, and colors. Some of them sparkled in the light like the glassy silica sheaths of diatom algae, and entire sections of the wall cast their hue into the water. Maggie walked slowly along the ledge and looked—up a row of colorless four-sided grains and down a row of colorless six-sided ones. From these clear grains she passed to translucent ones permeated by traces of white. The hint of white expanded to yield solid white grains with both rough and glossy faces. Next she passed pale green grains to dark green grains, arranged from transparent to opaque, from shiny to dusty. Some grains were irregular in shape whereas others were cut in symmetrical forms: fat ten-sided balls, steep eight-sided double pyramids, six-sided spikes and six-sided plates, round-cornered cubes, and clusters of flat bristles. The greens gave way to blues, the blues to wondrous violets and purples, and the purples to blacks. Beyond glimmering black crystals there were brown grains, then red ones, then orange ones.

Rensaleer was waiting for her here.

"These are the realgar crystals. Here, hold this." He handed her his cinnabar crystal, which she clumsily clasped in her claw. She felt awkward holding the crystal; even though her claws were long and slender, they seemed clumsy compared with Rensaleer's cushioning mitts.

Rensaleer crawled up the wall to the fifth cross thread, removed a grain, and returned.

"See, realgar has only one axis of twofold symmetry." He proceeded to rotate the grain in various arrangements to demonstrate its symmetry to Maggie.

Looking at the grain Rensaleer held, then at the one she held, then back again to the one Rensaleer held, and then back to hers, Maggie said, "Oh, yessss … I see," not really knowing if she did or not.

Rensaleer replaced the realgar crystal and began pacing. "Where to place this cinnabar?" he muttered. Stopping before Maggie he said, "Crystal form is most easily confused with the realgar. But look at its color."

Maggie looked at the red grain she held, up at the reddish-orange grain Rensaleer had just replaced, and then across the bright orange grains that were in a row beyond the realgar. Meanwhile, Rensaleer walked in the opposite direction. He stopped before a row of reddish cubes and octahedrons. "Really is closer in color to this cuprite." He returned to take the cinnabar from Maggie. "Also in its luster and translucency."

"Does it matter exactly where you put it?" Maggie asked.

Rensaleer's entire posture stiffened; his antennae became rigid. In a formal tone, each syllable distinct, he said, "With-out know-ing the el-e-ments of the ground we walk on, how can we e-ver know the stream in which we dwell?"

"Oh, I see," said Maggie softly.

Rensaleer's tone softened. "If I can determine the proper placement of these grains, perhaps, eventually, I shall see how the very substrates of the stream are arranged."

Rensaleer climbed up the row of cuprite crystals, crawled across the wall to the few realgar grains, crawled back to the cuprite, and then climbed down. "This is very difficult, you know," he said tensely. "This grain is igneous in origin, as is realgar. Cuprite is metamorphic. And look at its cleavage," he lifted his forebody to look over the row of cuprite, "at most poor octahedral, whereas cinnabar is perfect. Certainly closer to realgar." Rensaleer returned to the realgar and held the grains side by side. "But the color, the luster." He returned to the cuprite and studied several of these grains closely. "But no. Just no," he concluded. "Definitely is an igneous rock with prismatic cleavage—nothing changes that. Goes here, next to these realgars. I'm going to have to rearrange these." Rensaleer began to mutter to himself as he moved grains down one row, across one row, up two rows, then down again.

While Rensaleer rearranged, Maggie walked along the remainder of the wall, passing the oranges to reach the yellows. She wondered if she could know these grains as Rensaleer did—how they were alike, how they were different, where they came from, where they belonged. If she could learn the stream's elements, might she be able to see her way to the richest of foods?

"Ah, yes, my golden panel," Rensaleer said as he came up behind her at the far end of the wall. "Quite a few different types here—pyrite, muscovite, gold." He tapped the irregular, filigreed gold mass and then pulled away a few strands of algae that were tangled in it. "Haven't worked with them very much. Run across them occasionally, so I collect them. Hate to see an unfixed grain," he quipped as his hindlegs began to wander. "Do have to get them properly arranged one of these days. Anyway, I'll walk back with you to the inner stream—if you can wait while I get a bite."

At his lodgings, Rensaleer pulled some large pieces of debris from his food net with his mandibles and tossed the refuse into the current. Then, starting at the upper right corner, he began to eat every item that remained on the net: leaf fragments, green, blue-green, and yellow algae, bacteria, fungi, floc, silt, loose silk—all of it went straight into his mouth, where his mandibles crunched the conglomeration into a more compact, homogeneous mass.

Maggie watched his mandibles move quickly. At times one surface pounded the other when something that resisted gentler chewing came along. In very little time, Rensaleer had consumed everything on the net, every bit of it, some bits of which Maggie thought untasty and indigestible.

Once Rensaleer had finished his meal, he turned to pulling twigs and large leaf fragments off his lodgings. He moved from one activity to the next as if satiating himself on his pace. Some juicy, plump diatoms growing atop his shelter now came into sight. Maggie was tempted to stretch up and eat them, but she thought snacking on her new acquaintance's home would be rude.

"It's forever getting cluttered like this," Rensaleer said. "Goes with the territory."

"Why don't you move instream," Maggie suggested; "the leaf litter wouldn't be such a problem there."

"Too much current for my collection," he replied as he struggled with a large leaf wedged just inside the entrance of his lodge. "And too many other streamlings around to disrupt my work." Rensaleer freed the leaf from the entrance and threw it into the current. "Ready?"

"Quite," Maggie replied, her gills fatigued from beating the water for air.

Rensaleer led Maggie through a narrow valley that cut a path between some low hills. The knolls sheltered the valley from the current, and the sediment seemed contentedly undisturbed. The valley was a cul-de-sac, and when they reached its end, they ascended the gentle slope of the lowest of the hills. Coming to the crest of the rock, Rensaleer stopped abruptly. His hindlegs walked downstream until he was face to face with Maggie. "I know some stoneflies who live just downstream of here. Sometimes they find real gems. Want to go see if something new has washed in?" Rensaleer's antennae twitched in anticipation, and his hindlegs started walking back upstream. "They're very friendly."

Taken with Rensaleer's grain collecting, his enthusiasm infectious, Maggie agreed to accompany him. She was a bit hungry, though, not having had a full meal that morning, so she sampled the forage of the shallow hills as they walked.

The vegetation was quite lush. There were dark green *cladophora* trees, thick with plumose, cylindrical branches, and smaller, paler *stigeoclonium* bushes covered with thin, tapering twigs. Fat, golden diatoms hung overhead from arborescent stalks—crescent-shaped *cymbellas* and wedge-shaped *gomphonemas*—while below them the ground was carpeted with loosely affixed diatoms: narrow, elliptic *naviculas*; fat, oval *surirellas*; clusters of needle-like *synedra*; long chains of circular *melosira*. Thin, tangled strands of bright green *mougeotia* tumbled through the understory. Maggie moved from spot to spot tasting the forage, munching some *cymbellas* here, a few *naviculas* there. Yet nothing she found was very tasty. The algae grew large in these slow waters, but their walls were tough and their inners rather stale. All in all, the fare turned out to be quite bland. The forage instream wasn't as lush, but it certainly was tastier.

"You know," Rensaleer said catching up to Maggie at a spray of *gomphonema*, "a net is much more efficient. Don't have to spend time looking for food. Net collects all my food for me. Just have to keep an eye on it, so it doesn't overload."

"I don't mind spending the time looking for something that is especially tasty."

"Ah, food is food," Rensaleer said as they resumed walking together. "I'm not picky. Need my time for collecting."

"But there must be times that your net doesn't gather enough for you."

"I get what I need. Not the fattest midge, but all plumpness buys is trouble."

Maggie looked at Rensaleer's flat black eyes, which seemed painted on his yellow face. "You're not neglecting your diet purposely?" she admonished. She couldn't understand Rensaleer's apparent indifference to his proper nourishment.

"Won't be so tasty to a fish," he chirped.

"You won't be any less tasty to a dragonfly," Maggie retorted.

"Won't as likely be swept off the ground into the drift," Rensaleer returned.

This remark quieted Maggie for a moment; she didn't want to admit to her bad drifting habit.

"Being in the drift is not doom," she finally said; "one just needs to get one's claws back on the ground again."

"If one can overcome the strong currents," Rensaleer pointed out.

"The trick is in orienting yourself to dive back to the ground as soon as you see the opportunity to do so," Maggie told him.

"May be easy for you, but I'm not the swimmer you are."

Yet it was probably luck more than ease that allowed Maggie to see being in the drift as she did. Although there had been times when she doubted that she'd ever be able to regain her footing, she had not yet lost even a bristle.

"I've had to move my net a few times," Rensaleer volunteered after a few moments of silence. "In cold water season lived closer to the inner stream. Beginning of fast water season moved to where I am now. But moved because the current kept unfastening my collection."

"Even when one finds a good place, there's no guarantee that it will stay that way," Maggie said as they walked around a large log that lay in their path. "My experience has been that it doesn't." Maggie paused. Then she told Rensaleer her plan.

"I've been thinking—perhaps I'll travel from reach to reach, spending time where I find good forage, moving on if I don't."

"Traveling so much is dangerous," Rensaleer said with concern. "You'll pass through unfamiliar waters. You'll be vulnerable to predators."

"You travel about too, Rensaleer, in search of your grains."

"I look around the neighborhood. Don't travel to places unknown. Anyway, how do you know you'll find something better someplace else?"

"There must be richer patches than those I've found; I wouldn't want to miss them."

Maggie stopped in front of a pile of leaves. She looked toward a ridge in the shallows where the already weak current had dissipated and left scenic swirls of sand.

"What are you looking for that isn't here?" Rensaleer asked her.

"I'm not sure," Maggie replied. "I'll know better when I see it."

"How will you know you've found it if you don't know what it looks like?" Rensaleer asked.

"I'm not sure," Maggie confessed. "But what can one do when one's feeding ground is no longer rich? One has to find forage."

"Plenty of food here," Rensaleer said. "Good solid ground too," he added.

Maggie looked at him with disbelief. "In the stream, no rock is forever grounded."

"Oh yes, I know that," Rensaleer dismissed. "But I'd rather have my rock to stand on than be trying to settle on one unknown."

They were approaching the stoneflies' leaf pack. Leaves covered much of the ground, and peripheral waters were being pulled inward by a chute of faster flowing water. Not until Maggie and Rensaleer reached the cusp of the rock, though, could they see the pack.

A range of tall ridges ran perpendicular to the current and formed a dam. Logs that had been denied passage by the dam now provided a frame for the pack: the logs corralled drifting leaves and channeled the stream's waters, creating a perfect leaf jam. To Maggie and Rensaleer's right an enormous wood beam extended from the rock on which they stood to the high range of ridges that formed the pack's dam. Between where they stood and the dam, between the beam and as far into the shallows as Maggie could see, was a valley of leaves. What Maggie didn't see, though, were any stoneflies, for they lived within the basin of leaves.

"Hey Rennie!" a cheerful voice called out. "I found something for you." The voice was that of a robust stonefly who had spied their approach.

"I almost ate it," the creamy tan stonefly continued as he stepped down from the large wood beam. When he reached them, he spread the palps of his broad-toothed lower lip in a wide smile and gave Maggie a hearty hello.

The stonefly dwarfed Maggie and Rensaleer. Although not much longer than either of them, he was much broader and taller. His body seemed impenetrable, armored with three heavy rectangular shields that covered the back of his thorax. His abdomen was shorter than his thorax, but almost as wide, and was edged with small spines. Spines also covered his stout legs, which had largely concealed clusters of forked gills at their bases. The stonefly had long antennae and two long tail filaments, but his antennae and tail were much more rigid than were Maggie's. His head was narrow in comparison to the rest of his body, and his eyes were small.

"So what is it, Rennie?" asked the stonefly as he pulled out a translucent blue, cylindrical grain from under his wing pad and handed it to Rensaleer.

"Oh ... mmm ... yes ..." Rensaleer muttered, his attention immediately absorbed by the grain. He appraised it, turning it over and over in his bristly palm. "An apatite, like the other blue grain you showed me. But the other crystal was tabular, flat. Probably why you didn't recognize this one." As Rensaleer started to show the grain to Maggie, he added, "Oh, Maggie, this is Rudy—Rudy, Maggie."

"Hello, hello," Rudy greeted Maggie enthusiastically. "When did you move into the neighborhood?"

"I arrived just last night."

"It's a great place! Great place!" Rudy lifted his head and looked from side to side, nodding. "We've been living here for four full night lights now. It's taken some work to get the leaf pack going, but we're bringing it into full production. We've got a great crop growing. Come on," he said, resting his claw on Maggie's wing pad, "let me show you around."

Rensaleer motioned with his right antenna that they should go on without him. "Going to see if anyone else has something for me."

Rudy led Maggie up the beam that extended to the dam. As they walked Rudy told her, "There are about one hundred of us stoneflies in this contingent. We came here when the leaves of our childhood grounds were exhausted. It's been a great place. How did you meet old Rennie there?"

"We met this morning, near the inner stream. He was collecting, and I came upon him just as he found a … I forget. A very nice red grain. He brought me to see his collection."

"He's a great fly," nodded Rudy, "and he really knows his grains. I've tried to get him to join the pack, but he only has time for those crystals. He's helped us out, though. Told us not to waste our time on the outer stream," Rudy pointed toward the shallows of the shallows; "said the sediment there indicated frequent stagnation, so we'd never get a good crop going."

Rudy stopped walking. The beam had brought them high above the leaf pack. "When we first got here," Rudy said, "the leaf pack was well above this beam. See where the cleft in the dam is?" He pointed to a gap high in the ridge, almost at the top of the stream. "That used to be our output chute! There's still a lot of material to be worked, but we've actually begun pulling in leaves from the margin. We use those leaves as our roof. Yes, we get three bits with one bite—have a roof, get the muck washed off, and invigorate the crop. Yes, we've got quite the operation. But come on, you can't see it from here." Rudy laughed and headed back down the beam.

Maggie followed Rudy to an opening in the wall of leaves. They entered a dark tunnel, where Maggie couldn't see a thing, so she followed Rudy by touching her antennae to his tail. Her gills grazed the tunnel's walls.

Maggie had never voyaged into a leaf pack before. How strange it felt to be so enclosed. The pack seemed a living being as it bobbed in the current as an intact mass. With water resonating in the passages and chambers of its complex maze, the pack even seemed to have a voice.

"These are the holding bays," Rudy told her as they walked through the tunnel.

Once away from the periphery of the pack, Maggie heard the voices of what she took to be other stoneflies. She also began to hear a constant, encompassing, "grrch, grrch, grrch."

"What is that?" Maggie asked Rudy.

"What?"

"That sound ... it sounds like the 'quusch' of fast waters, but there's more of a 'grr' to it."

Rudy stopped to listen and after a few moments started to laugh. "Those are the macromacerators. Come on, we're almost there." Within a few more leaf lengths, they entered a large, noisy, and busy chamber. There were stoneflies everywhere, big-bodied stoneflies, pulling leaf fragments sometimes twenty times their size to their stations on the transfer chute.

"The oldest of our clan work here in the maceration room," Rudy told her. "We call them the macromacerators. They take the raw materials and prep them for the rest of the pack. The pace is set in here."

These large fragments of decaying vegetable matter, commonly called leaf litter, were far from waste. They were coated with a rich, nutritious assortment of bacteria and fungi that flourished by turning a leaf back into its elements, elements that, in turn, fostered new life. Rudy and his clan were another cog in the recycling process. Feeding on the leaves, bacteria, and fungi, the macromacerators broke large leaf fragments into smaller fragments and passed these smaller fragments on to smaller stoneflies, who performed the next phase of the cycle.

Maggie and Rudy meandered through the chamber, Rudy saying hello to his compatriots as he passed them, patting wing pads and grasping foreclaws, receiving nods and hellos in return.

"Is this where you feed?" queried Maggie.

"Well, sometimes, but more often I stop in the mastication room for a quick bite. This was my last shop before promotion. I'm primarily a runner now. The macromacerators set the pace, but because we're one operation, we've got to keep all the shops running in sync. So I move back and forth, checking all points of the process, telling the macromacerators when to slow down, the micromacerators when to speed up—making sure everybody's happy."

"Quite a job," Maggie said, "to make everybody happy."

"It's not that hard," Rudy replied, "for we're all working together here, making sure everyone is well taken care of. Sometimes, sure, there are personality differences. So, you tell Sally to go help Freddy, and tell Rickie to close his trap. But we're all streamlings here, working for the same thing."

"What's that?" Maggie asked.

"The health and prosperity of our community, of our children to be," Rudy sang out. "And we're working not only for our own kind but for the stream. Yes, our plant produces food and nutrients for streamlings much smaller than ourselves. Taking the old from the stream, making food for the new—if we didn't maintain our vigilance, what a pileup of rotting vegetable matter there would be!"

Maggie was impressed. To what finer goal could one aspire than finding one's sustenance not only in feeding toward one's own adulthood but also in contributing toward the fulfillment of others?

"Come along, I'll show you the rest of this operation," Rudy said happily as he gazed at Maggie's face.

They walked along the bank of the chute that carried macerated leaf fragments to the next chamber. The chute created a small current that Maggie found refreshing. Even in the large maceration chamber, the enclosed waters of the leaf pack were stuffy.

"This is the diminution room," Rudy gestured in a sweeping motion as they entered the next chamber. Here the stoneflies were smaller, closer to Maggie in size, and the atmosphere a bit lighter without large leaves being carried about. "This is where we usually have our backups. Sometimes I think it's because these fellows chatter so much. They're the micromacerators; we call them the micromacs for short. They feed on the smaller leaf plates that the macromacs have produced. The micromacs expose and soften fresh surfaces of the leaves for bacteria and fungi to colonize."

Next, Rudy led Maggie through a tunnel that circumvented the holding reservoir, which separated the micromacs' chamber and the last feeding room. "The slurry in the reservoir is just too dense to walk through," Rudy said. "After the macromacs and micromacs, not much of a crop is left on the leaves," he explained, "so we give the leaves about two night lights in the reservoir to reinvigorate the crop. We have agitators in there, mostly midges, who mix the porridge while it's stewing, and I—and the other runners, of course—go in periodically to make quality control checks. When the leaves are properly seasoned, we move them on to the masticators."

Rudy and Maggie emerged into the last chamber, which was full of young stoneflies busily chewing. The masticators were the smallest of the contingent; in time, they would grow to be micromacs and then, eventually, macromacs. They performed the final stage of processing: chewing the leaf fragments thoroughly and sending them on as minute particles.

"We make sure the masticators get a rich diet, so they'll get a good start," Rudy proudly told Maggie. "Perhaps reworking the old to become the new isn't the most glamorous of callings, but we're rewarded in knowing how essential a service we provide for the stream.

"Well, that's the tour," Rudy sighed. "We can take a shortcut back out." They traveled a tunnel that had a steep slope, and soon they were on the beam from which they had entered the pack.

"I wonder where Rensaleer has taken off to," Maggie said as they walked down the beam to the upstream end of the pack. She finally spied Rensaleer's lanky greenish body poking among some leaves and pointed him out to Rudy. They walked up behind him.

"Any gee-whizzes?" asked Rudy.

"No, not really," Rensaleer answered, turning around. "Did find these two microlite crystals." He held two greenish-black grains forward for Maggie and Rudy to see. "Have several black octahedrals of various lusters. Been trying to resolve their placement. Perhaps if I determine the quality that defines these microlites, I'll be able to place my spinels, magnetites, and chromites." Rensaleer's hindlegs started to wander. "Okay if I excuse myself from our trip instream, Maggie? I'd like to take these home."

"Why you heading instream?" Rudy asked Maggie.

"She's looking for a good patch," Rensaleer answered for her.

"So, you're looking for a good patch," Rudy nodded his head in understanding. "They can be hard to find. Yes, the stream can seem really wanting at times. But you know, Maggie, that is what we've made here: a good patch, rich and rejuvenating. You could fit right in, Maggie. You could be a grate scraper."

"Well, um," Maggie hesitated, finding Rudy's invitation warm but grate scraping not particularly appealing. "I'll think about it. It's a bit different from what I've had in mind."

"Well, go ahead and ruminate, but we've got the best show in the reach," Rudy told her assuredly, grasping her wing pad.

"See you later, macerator," Rensaleer said to Rudy. "And you come visit, Maggie."

"I will. And I'll come see you too, Rudy. But for now, I'm off to find some greens."

And so the group broke up, each going his own way: Rensaleer to his collection, Rudy back to his pack, and Maggie to look for some good, solid, ruminating grounds.

CHAPTER THREE

THE WAY OF THE PACK

Heading instream from Rudy's took Maggie over some rough terrain: several more logs barricaded the leaf pack or, one could say, maintained it. She hadn't thought of asking Rensaleer or Rudy for a route, for what could be more straightforward, besides heading upstream or down, than heading instream from the shallows.

Finally, after climbing over logs and jagged rock rubble, crawling along barky crevices and around dense clumps of leaves, Maggie reached what for a mayfly is solid ground—a continuous expanse of rocky terrain. Here, there were broad stones covered with fertile fields and mossy thickets—not sand, leaves, and logs. Here, there was a full-bodied current, not too fast but far from slow. Yes, how nice, Maggie thought as she began to graze on crisp diatoms and tender green shoots. This was where she belonged. She grazed far into the night light, until her stomach was full. Then she found a comfortable leeward crevice and went to sleep.

When Maggie woke, she found the contentment of her fullness had been replaced by a nagging doubt. She looked around. Were these the rocks she sought? They were comfortable enough and provided some tasty forage, but was this the best she could find? Yet should she wander in search of a patch that might or might not be? She grazed inattentively for a while and then decided to go see Rensaleer.

Reaching Rensaleer's retreat, Maggie found it empty. He must had left recently, though, for only a few morsels adhered to his food net. Maggie fluttered her gills to draw in the air that diffused into the stream from the other world. She sent a plum of grains into the current.

Thinking that Rensaleer might be working on his collection, Maggie walked across the basin and down the path they had taken the day before. She looked over the wall of grains in search of him, but, apparently, he was not there.

The wall billowed softly, rhythmically, in the gentle current, its points glistening brightly in the light. Each grain was in order, fixed in its place with a name and a history. And Rensaleer, being keeper of the wall, he was given a place too. What an amazing wall, Maggie thought. And if there was an order to these grains, some principle to how they all fit together, wasn't there a place for everything? And could she come to know this very pattern of the stream's mesh?

As Maggie turned to leave, she heard Rensaleer call her. She looked back at the wall, but Rensaleer's thin body blended into the wall so well she couldn't see him.

"Here," Rensaleer called, "in the violets."

Maggie finally spotted him between a row of deeply colored hexagons and a row of slightly more transparent cubes. "There you are!" she said. "Have you found something new?"

"Haven't been out yet," he replied, starting toward her.

"I thought I might give Rudy's offer a try," she told him.

"Ah. Good. You'll be a grate scraper." Rensaleer climbed down from the wall. "I'll accompany you."

Rensaleer led the way up the path to his lodgings. When Maggie stepped out from behind him and into the basin, she gasped. His net was gone!

"Happens all the time," Rensaleer told her nonchalantly as he inspected the damage. His hindlegs walked downstream, and he looked at Maggie with his right eyes. "Someone passes by, takes a look around, and then gobble, gobble, gobble—" his hindlegs meandered the hemisphere back upstream, "gone. Sometimes quite a find, I imagine." His left eyes now looked at her.

"That's just terrible," Maggie said, "someone taking your net."

"Oh, takes only a few minutes to fix," Rensaleer dismissed.

With the silk he produced in his salivary glands, Rensaleer first reinforced the heavy silk ropes that extended upstream from the entrance of the lodge. These ropes anchored his lodge to the ground and nearby brush. Next, slightly upstream of the tent's entrance, Rensaleer formed the frame of his food net by stretching strands between the anchor lines. Continuing with the main body of the net, he spun and strung a few thin threads across the frame's top and then a few from its top to its bottom. Then he added a few horizontal threads across the bottom and a few more vertical ones to the sides. In this manner he wove in toward the center, placing strands in rough parallel. Once he had the rudiment of the net, he embellished upon it, making some large gaps smaller and some thin threads heavier.

Maggie watched Rensaleer's quick, jerky movements as he built his new net. Whereas his collection was maintained with the utmost fastidiousness, his food net was constructed solely to meet its basic requirements. Although not a net builder, Maggie could see that in his hasty construction Rensaleer left large gaps through which the fine, richer food bits he should be eating would pass while large, less nutritious chunks would remain stuck.

"There now. Done," Rensaleer said as he anchored down the last thread.

As they crossed the sediment valley, Maggie asked, "If your net gets stolen, why don't you replace it when you plan on staying home?"

"Rather build another one than tie myself down."

"You're not losing just your net, though," Maggie said with a touch of consternation, "but also all the energy you used to build it."

"Aah, doesn't take much to maintain me."

"But in the long run, Rensaleer, in the long run—your future depends on your mass."

"I'll make the weight."

To Maggie this somehow didn't seem enough; Rensaleer should want more. "What about the other world?" she asked.

"The other world? Hmm. ... Don't ignore it. Just don't focus my attention there"

Rensaleer stopped and suggested they take a different route to Rudy's. Instead of walking to the valley's end, they climbed a ridge closer to the stream's margin.

"Anyway," Rensaleer said when they reached the top of the rise, "who knows what best nourishes for the other world? Say you find that patch you're looking for—what if all along the way you were passing by good forage?"

"Well, one day I may find the richest."

"Maybe. All depends on how much you want to rely on 'may.' My net works fine. My collection, though, that fulfills me. My grains give me pleasure, make me useful." Rensaleer stretched across a trench into which Maggie, without his flexibility, had to descend. "I come from a long line of grain keepers," he told her when she reemerged; "grain distinction is in my blood. Without my occupation, I'd be just another indistinctive, net-spinning midge."

Maggie envied Rensaleer this, for indeed, she was just another pedestrian mayfly. When she was younger, it seemed that with each molt she was growing rapidly toward something. She had expected she'd travel the stream unharmed, growing bigger and wiser along the way. But now her course seemed more a meander, and the dreams of her early molts seemed buried beneath the sediment, like her last home.

Rensaleer turned to looking for grains. With his face to the ground, he walked along the sinuous contours of sediment that covered these low-lying ridges. Maggie poked around too, hoping to find some grain of distinction that would ignite Rensaleer's enthusiasm. A spiny, green *tetraedron* ball tumbled past her.

When they reached the leaf pack, no one was in sight. "I guess I'll go in and look for Rudy," Maggie said.

"I'll go on then," Rensaleer told her as his hindlegs wandered until they were immediately downstream of his head. His body formed a circle. "Planned to go a bit instream of here." His legs walked back upstream until his body straightened out. "Stream changes—different size grains." His legs continued upstream and stopped when his body formed a hook. "See you later." With that, his forelegs led him through an *S* that straightened out as he headed instream.

"Bye!" Maggie called, waving an antenna in farewell. "I'll keep my eyes open for crystals."

Maggie walked to the tunnel she and Rudy had entered the day before. When she reached the entrance, though, she recalled how dark and circuitous the passageway was. Unsure of whether she could find her way through on her own, Maggie poked her head into the tunnel and called, "Hello. Hello." But her voice did not carry; it only blended with the sounds of water echoing in the passageways. "What did I expect," she asked herself, "a welcoming committee?"

After a few minutes of sitting and humphing, and seeing that Rensaleer was already out of sight, Maggie headed into the dark tunnel. With her antennae stretched out before her, she proceeded slowly, feeling the walls of the tunnel ahead. Repeatedly her antennae plunged into large pits in the tunnel's irregular surface. Each time this happened, she probed the pit with an antenna to make sure it wasn't a turn in the tunnel.

It was in one of these pits that bristles touched Maggie's bristles and sent an instantaneous chill throughout her body. She froze. Then, through the sound of her lymph pounding, Maggie heard a voice come out of the darkness.

"Are you lost?" it asked gently.

"Yes, I am," Maggie replied weakly, the joints in her legs about to give way. "I'm looking for Rudy."

"Straight ahead," said a large stonefly, coming out from the alcove in which he had been standing. Then realizing that Maggie was a bit shaken, he added, "I'll take you."

"I'd appreciate that. This tunnel is very confusing."

"Ah, not once you know it," the stonefly said reassuringly.

Reviving some from her fright, Maggie asked, "What are you doing out here?"

"I'm on sentry duty. In case any unwanteds try to get in," he explained.

"Oh. Well. I have an invitation—to come join the pack," Maggie identified herself.

"Good. We can always use a scraper. The more we put in, the more we get out.

"Here we are," said the sentry as they approached the light of the macromacs' chamber. "Rudy is in there somewhere. Others will direct you. I have to return to my post."

"Thank you very much." Maggie said and nodded goodbye.

Maggie stood at the entrance to the cavernous maceration chamber and looked over the corps of working stoneflies but did not see Rudy. Instead, she saw a mass of his kind: broad, hard-backed stoneflies foraging together, in harmony, so that they all would be fulfilled.

A mature stonefly, one who would soon emerge as an adult in the other world, entered the chamber at the output chute and initiated a wave of communication that brought everyone to a halt. The stoneflies broke into small groups and began to chat. Maggie saw that this might be a good time to find Rudy. She walked up to the closest group of stoneflies and greeted them. "Hi there," she said, feeling quite dwarfed by their collective size. "I'm looking for Rudy. Have any of you seen him?"

"He was here just awhile ago," a stubby-palped stonefly answered, lifting his head to look around the chamber.

"Are you the mayfly who's thinking about joining the pack?" another in the group asked amiably.

"Yes. I've decided to."

"That's great," the stoneflies commended her, giving her their toothy grins.

"The pack will be quite a change for me," Maggie told them. "I've never scraped grates before," she said, "nor can I say that I've spent much time in such a well-sheltered residence," she added, looking up to where shafts of light poked through the dark, leafy ceiling. "But I'll give it a try."

"That's the attitude," said a particularly brawny stonefly. "Once you become accustomed to life here, you'll find you like it, and soon you'll find you wouldn't have it any other way."

"There's Rudy," said the stonefly who had been looking for him. He pointed out Rudy to Maggie. Rudy was talking to the stonefly who had initiated the work stoppage.

"Well, I guess I'll go find out where I'm supposed to start. See you later."

When Rudy saw Maggie, he greeted her heartily. "Maggie! Good to see you."

"Hello, Rudy. I've come to try out grate scraping."

"Great! Great!" Clasping Maggie's wing pad with one foreclaw and his companion's foreleg with his other, Rudy said, "Maggie, I'd like you to meet Mary. Mary is a runner, like me, so you'll be seeing a lot of her."

"Pleased to meet you," Maggie said.

"Glad to see you here," returned Mary; "we can really use someone with your talents. Grate scraping requires skills that we stoneflies just can't manage."

"Well, where do I start?" asked Maggie.

"I'll take you there," said Rudy. Then turning to Mary to finish their conversation he said, "They're just going to have to wait until we can make space in the holding bin. It's not the micromacs' fault that oak leaves don't yield a good crop."

"Yeah, yeah," nodded Mary, unhappy about the message she was about to deliver. Then in a cheerier tone she said, "See you later, Maggie."

"Come with me," Rudy said as he released Maggie's wing pad.

"This position is made for you," he told her as they walked. "You get to move around a lot—within the pack, of course. I'll show you where all the grates are now. You'll be operating pretty independently, although from time to time we'll have you move to where the operation needs you."

At the beginning and end of each transfer chute were grates that caught leaf chunks too large to go on to the next chamber. These grates were remarkable structures made of fine wood beams and heavy leaf veins laced together with silk. Maggie wouldn't work alone at these grates. At each there was one or two micromacs who removed and macerated the morsels that were too large to pass through. It would be

Maggie's job to clean these grates of the bacteria and fungi that flourished on them, for if these microbes went unheeded, they would clog the grates' openings.

And so Maggie began her day in the micromacs' chamber, negotiating footings on a mesh that she wasn't made to walk on and scraping bacteria and fungi from a narrow, woody substrate. Maggie fed diligently, though, part of the grand process that turned leaf litter into food for herself, for the stoneflies, for the stream. She pulled her scoop-like palps together, scraping the viscous mass from the mesh, and brought her palps to her lips. Her lips raked the food into her mouth, and then, swallowing, she stretched her palps out again.

Maggie worked alongside Jeannie and Dougie, the two micromacs on screen duty. Apparently, their assignment wasn't considered one of the more desirable, for one spent more time removing leaf fragments from the mesh than eating them.

At what Jeannie and Dougie called rectime, Rudy came by to see how Maggie's morning had gone.

"My claws get caught a lot, and my palps ache from scraping along these narrow bars, but it's fun having Jeannie and Dougie's company," she told him.

"Yes, it sure does feel good, doesn't it, to feed alongside friends, foraging toward fulfillment together," Rudy said with understanding. "Out there, in the stream, alone, unsheltered, a disconnected streamling—a streamling who at any moment can be lost to the current—you can never be sure of your grounding. That's what makes this pack great. Here, you belong to something: a firm foundation of purpose and support; a home among friends who always appreciate your efforts and are happy to see you every day that they do. Yes, this is what we have in the pack, what we want, what we need." Rudy had become so moved speaking of the goodness of the pack that he had to stop speaking for a moment. When he resumed, he changed the topic. "We have lots of activities planned for rectime. We have a sing, decorative leaf excising, swimming, four-legged crawl races—you'd probably like swimming. It's my favorite." Without waiting for a response, Rudy tugged Maggie's foreleg. "Come along."

Rudy led Maggie to a pool just upstream and to the shallows of the leaf pack. Many stoneflies were already there, and most were chasing one another in a game of tag.

Maggie did love to swim. At her first home there had been a deep pool in which she would glide just above the surface of the streambed, riding the currents. The pool here was very different, though. Being in the shallows, its waters were still, and its floor was silty and covered with quagmires of tangled algae. Maggie sank every time she touched the bottom, and when she vented her gills, she covered herself with sediment.

At the far edge of the pool, out of the way of those playing tag, Maggie glided through the waters. She flipped over in a turn and coasted back along the edge. One flick of her abdomen sent her halfway across the pool. She flipped over again and was gliding back across the pool when suddenly she was knocked to the ground.

"Oh my, I'm so sorry," apologized the micromac who had crashed into her back. "Are you all right?"

"Yes, I think so," Maggie replied from the cloud of dust she had raised upon impact. She flexed her back to make sure she wasn't hurt.

"How about playing tag with us then?" invited the micromac.

"Thanks, but I don't think so."

"Oh, come on," the small stonefly tugged her with his words.

"Well, I—" Maggie hesitated.

"Oh, come on," he pulled, "we'll be on the same team."

Maggie nodded a half-hearted consent and swam with this little stonefly, Freddie, to the group playing tag. "We're in, we're in!" Freddie shouted to the players, and he was immediately tagged "it."

Maggie played the game well. Although she had never considered herself a good swimmer, compared with the stoneflies, she was very agile. They played until Mary came to call them back to the pack.

"I wish we could stay out longer," Maggie said to Freddie as they walked toward their stations together.

"Yes, but it's time to get back to feeding. I'm always ready to return to work now, ever since I got these." He grabbed one of his small wing pads. "Remember, the more we put in, the more we get out."

Freddie and Maggie parted at the grate where Maggie had been working. Dougie and Jeannie had already returned. They had gone to creative leaf excising, for they both had been a bit hungry, and one got to eat what one cut out. Dougie pulled out a lacy square of leaf from under his wing pad to show Maggie. Most of the leaf was gone; it had been turned into an intricate pattern of delicately framed holes. The leaf reminded Maggie of some days in the cold-water season when the light entered the stream through a lace of ice and danced upon the substrate.

The three settled down to work and fed for a long time, stopping only occasionally to let their stomachs catch up with their mouths. Maggie listened to the rhythmical "grrch, grrch, grrch," of the chamber as she scraped.

When Mary called an end to the day's foraging, Maggie decided to go outside for a breath of fresh, running water. As she started for the tunnel, though, Jeannie grabbed her hindleg and said, "It's this way to convergence."

"I thought I'd just go out for a while, for some fresh water," Maggie explained.

"Oh, not now. You can't miss convergence."

So Maggie went along. A short passageway led them into a large, vaulted chamber that was filling with all the members of the leaf pack. Maggie could now see the other members of the group who weren't stoneflies. There were a few midges, who worked in the holding reservoir, and a few beetle larvae, who, like the stoneflies, shredded leaves. She also saw Freddie, who waved at her, and Rudy, who was in a huddle with Mary and some other macromacs who Maggie took to be the other runners.

Once pack members had stopped entering the chamber from its various portals, someone started to sing and immediately was joined by the entire group:

> *Large to small and small to large,*
> *we share the leaves of the stream's waters.*
> *Growing, knowing, side by side,*
> *the pack is our home in the waters.*

They all broke into a cheer at the end of the verse and then started singing it again, after which they sang another stanza:

> *When I'm unsure, I ask myself,*
> *what is the way of a good leaf pack?*
> *Knowing we're growing side by side,*
> *for we have a home in the leaf pack.*

Again, they all clapped for themselves and for one another. Then they all quieted down.

"First item on the agenda," announced one of the runner stoneflies, "is to welcome our new scraper, Maggie."

Jeannie and Dougie waved their antennae high to direct the group's attention to Maggie. The group gave her a welcoming round of applause.

"We hope you feel right at home here, Maggie. I've heard you worked quite diligently today. That's an effort we all appreciate." The group gave Maggie an encouraging round of applause.

"Now, turning to other items—we had a bit of disharmony today due to poor leaf quality in the mastication chamber. Tomorrow, we'll set up a program of leaf rotation in the input bay in order to provide a better mix of leaves. But for now, macerators, you'll have to slow down a bit."

There was a fair amount of grumbling in response.

"Does anyone want to contribute?" admonished the runner stonefly.

No one spoke.

"I'm sure you all thoroughly understand the situation. Now, what else has been going on today?"

One stonefly waved her antennae and told the group the winners of the four-legged races. There were several categories because for each of the fore and mid, mid and hind, and fore and hind legged races, there was the macromac, micromac, and masticator division, as well as the opens. When the stonefly finished her reporting of winners, Mary waved her antennae and told the group that tomorrow there would be synchronized line dancing at rectime. From the murmurs, Maggie gathered this was a popular activity. When no more antennae or forelegs bid attention, the moderator resumed.

"We decided last night to continue our discussion on differences in head size, with tonight's discussion question being, 'Why do craneflies have such small heads?' Has anyone had any thoughts on the matter?"

Maggie had never thought of asking herself this before.

"Well, I was thinking," said one stonefly quite hesitantly, "it's not exactly that their heads are so small than it is that their bodies are so big." A few in the assembly chuckled. "I mean," stammered the stonefly, "if they were the size of a midge, their heads wouldn't be so small."

"Good point," a midge piped in.

So encouraged, the stonefly added, "Perhaps the question, then, is better stated as 'Why do craneflies have such big bodies?'"

"No changing the question," sang out several stoneflies.

The stonefly who had been speaking spread his palps in a frown.

"I think craneflies have such small heads so that they can retract them," another stonefly suggested. "They do have a habit of doing so."

Many of the stoneflies nodded in agreement and began to exchange comments on the strange habits of the craneflies. Although most craneflies were leaf eaters like the stoneflies, that was where their similarities ended. Craneflies were legless, sluggish, and not very social, often withdrawing their heads if one bumped into them. None had ever joined the pack, preferring instead to operate small, dense leaf packs individually. This predilection caused the stoneflies to question the craneflies' motivation, for a cranefly in a one-larva operation certainly couldn't be as productive as the stoneflies in their pack. Yet craneflies certainly put on the weight to show that they were feeding well. This observation had led some stoneflies to speculate that the craneflies were stripping the leaf litter bare, gorging themselves while not leaving even one fungal spore to reseed a leaf.

"I think craneflies have small heads because in the other world they have small heads!" someone shouted out above the murmuring. Many of the stoneflies began giggling.

"I think they have small heads because they feed on smaller morsels than we do," said one of the runners quite calmly.

This point brought a lot of mumbling accord, for what better defines one's form than the function one is meant to fulfill? Once the group quieted down, the moderator asked, "Are there any more ideas?"

Maggie heard some "well ... umm ... no's" and saw some heads nodding. After discussing the proposed alternatives a bit further, the assembly agreed that craneflies have small heads because they eat small morsels of food.

"Suggestion for tomorrow night's discussion?" asked the moderator.

"Why do dragonflies have such big heads?" someone called out.

"That will be an easy one," Jeannie whispered to Maggie. Then the group broke out in song again:

Rest ye well my fellows,
safely in the pack,
softly on your pillow,
friends you'll never lack.

Work we for tomorrow,
dreams we share tonight.
Fulfillment is our motto,
someday in our great flight.

With the end of the song, the gathering was called to a close. Stoneflies began filing out of the chamber.

"Come along with us," Dougie invited Maggie; "there's plenty of room in our cubby for you."

As they settled down in a cozy chamber not far from the convergence chamber, Maggie thought about the craneflies and their heads some more. Small heads and large bodies—why were their bodies so large? So soft-skinned were they, like Rensaleer. Such a tasty treat the fish must find them—large and soft and without legs. What a strange creature. But as adults, what were they like? Maggie, of course, had never seen an adult cranefly, but they must have wings, she thought, and perhaps legs too. And perhaps their little heads turned into big heads and their big bodies into little bodies? No, Maggie shook her head in drowsiness, that didn't make sense. But perhaps they changed a lot, for unlike her and the stoneflies, who gradually became adults inside their larval skins, the craneflies would go into a long pupal sleep during which they would completely change into their adult form.

Looking at Dougie and seeing him still awake, Maggie asked, "Do you think craneflies have such small heads as adults?"

"Why don't you suggest your question for a discussion at tomorrow's convergence," Dougie recommended.

"But what do you think about craneflies?" asked Maggie.

After a few moments he said, "Most flies have small heads; craneflies just happen to have large bodies. I guess in the other world they're large flies. But have the group discuss it; I'm sure we'll come up with the answer."

It was time to go to sleep. Maggie waved her gills slowly, evenly, in rhythm to the melody of the stream passing through the tunnels and chambers of the leaf pack. As she fell asleep, she imagined that day when wings would take her on a limitless flight through the denselessness of the world of air, a flight in the life-giving light of the other world. Dreaming of that day, she could almost feel her body lifting from the chamber, floating formless through the waters of the stream, and at the border of water and air, escaping into the other world. That day. A day. So brief. One day to have all those things.

CHAPTER FOUR

THE FOOD OF THE UPPER ROCK

The next day Maggie grazed with another team of stoneflies, and at rectime she went with these new acquaintances to the synchronized line dance. The dance was great fun, although she, as well as many other participants, received some scrapes and bruises. Particularly on hindleg kicks, many suffered blows to the abdomen from neighboring dancers. And during turns, one risked getting tail whipped. Yet everyone danced in good spirits, apologizing for or accepting the damage incurred.

Even before dancing, though, Maggie didn't feel well. When she returned to feeding, scraping the porridge of fine organic floc, bacteria, and fungi from the grates, she realized what was wrong: there were no fresh algae in her diet. So when it came time for the end-of-foraging assembly, Maggie told her companions that she was going outside for a while, to forage the algae that grew in the light of the upper rock. They insisted she not go, though, for one should never miss convergence. So Maggie forwent her foraging foray and attended the convergence. First she listened to "large to small and small to large" and then to a discussion of why dragonflies have big heads. "The better to eat you with, my dear," poked Jeannie.

There was also a discussion regarding a tube-case caddisfly who had arrived during the day's foraging and sought to join the pack.

"Remember what happened the last time we had a couple of those fellows in the pack?" a macromac reminded the group. "They kept removing leaves from the output chutes to freshen up those vain leaf cases they wrap around their abdomens."

"And those cases!" another stonefly took over. "Those cases were like a pile of logs in the middle of the aisle! I was forever banging my legs on them."

"Yes, a pile," the first stonefly returned, "because one always ran into those caddisflies in a throng—they were so cliquish, as if they weren't even a part of the pack."

"And they masticated when they were supposed to be macerating," a third stonefly said quickly, barely audible. This was an infraction one did not even want to be guilty of conceiving for it reflected such a repugnant absence of conscience.

The assembly agreed to deny the caddisfly admission to the pack, feeling that a fellow who always wore his own case would only insulate himself from the group's welfare.

Someone called out, "Hey, tomorrow let's discuss why caddisflies have such itty, bitty eyes." Several stoneflies seconded this motion.

The group then sang:

Rest ye well my fellows,
safely in the pack,
softly on your pillow,
friends you'll never lack.

Work we for tomorrow,
dreams we share tonight.
Fulfillment is our motto,
someday in our great flight.

When the song came to a close, Rudy was at Maggie's side. Apparently one of Maggie's coworkers had spoken to him. "I hear you're yearning for some green stuff," he said sympathetically.

"Yes, I am."

"We all have different tastes, don't we? Yes, the stream is full of all sorts." Rudy cocked his head. "Some like leaf litter, some like the green stuff, some even have a yen for floating flakes of floc. It's amazing, though, how we all fit together to keep the stream running, all an important cog. How the pack could stay together if we all were wandering over rock tops looking for algae, I don't know. But you want some greens!" He rested his claw on Maggie's wing pad. "Well, you know, there are great greens on the rocks at our instream border. Why don't you forage there during rectime tomorrow."

"I'll try it," Maggie agreed.

"Good." Rudy patted Maggie's wing pad. "Now we both better rest up well."

In their cozy cubby, Maggie nestled down and bid good dreams to Jeannie, Dougie, and the other micromacs there.

The cubby was one of many small, round chambers linked together by one of many corridors that radiated out from the assembly chamber. In the pre-sleep quiet, questions wafted into Maggie's chamber on the melodious current. Why do caddisflies have such small eyes? Why do dragonflies have such big eyes? With its many eyes, does the pack see more? Maggie wondered. Why don't we each have many eyes, all over our bodies, so that we might see in all directions at once? Because then, she answered herself, our skin would be a tussle of wanting to go in different directions. Maggie thought of Teresa, who had no eyes at all, and while Maggie wasn't looking, sleep floated into the chamber and gently overtook her.

The next day Maggie moved to a grate in the macromacs' chamber. Being around these robust fellows made her feel part of a great, invincible working machine. With the drone of "grrch, grrch, grrch" surrounding her, she scraped the grates. Yes, they all worked for the day that the macromacs would emerge and produce more masticators. The other world was the zenith of the cycle, where old gave way to new. With this continuity, there would always be stoneflies ready to turn leaf litter into fine detritus, mayflies to remove algae from rocks to make room for more growth, and midges to burrow into the sand and return to the waters the rich nutrients that had been lost to the sediments. Each was a cog in the working of the stream; each had one's purpose to fulfill; each was without ambiguity as to the value of one's place. And ultimately, each was responsible for replacing oneself, so that the stream would keep functioning properly, running smoothly, providing them the home they all needed.

As Rudy had suggested, at rectime Maggie parted with her company and made her way to the instream border of the leaf pack. She readily negotiated the tunnel that had intimidated her just two days before, so accustomed she had already become to the dark, narrow passageways. Soon she emerged into the open, and even the relatively slow current of the margin brought a gust of fresh water. Maggie faced upstream, stretched her gills out in the water, and shook herself.

So refreshed, Maggie hastened to look for some greens. But the ground she traversed was sparsely populated by algae; instead, it was cluttered with leafy and sandy debris. Unappetizing strands of spindly *mougeotia* and beady *anabaena* wrapped around the barren branches of the numerous logs. When Rudy came to fetch her, Maggie had found only one cottony cloud of tender, green *spirogyra* to eat.

Maggie returned to grate scraping, but she knew her appetite for greens had not been at all appeased. She pulled some small leaf fragments from the grate and chewed them slowly. Yes, here there was food, much food, but it was without any flavor, as if some vital element were missing. What Maggie wanted was food like algae, food that took elements from the stream and with the light of the other world put these elements together into something new, something fresh, something vital. So after convergence, Maggie told Rudy that she wanted to take a trip to the inner stream.

"Wasn't there any good food on our borders?" Rudy asked, his antennae peaked questioningly.

"I think I can find a much better spot instream," Maggie told him.

"Oh yes," he nodded in understanding; "that patch where the pabulum is rich and the sediment scarce, which is always full and never in senescence." Rudy laughed. "Yes, aren't we all looking for that idealized place?"

Are we all? wondered Maggie.

"Well, whatever you want," Rudy said. His voice rung with disappointment. "But you know, that's what we're working to build here: a rich feeding ground, solid and rejuvenating, in which we can all find our sustenance. Alone, none of us can cultivate a patch that will be lasting."

"But still, I need a greener diet," Maggie said.

Sighing, Rudy reached up and pulled down an elm leaf that dangled from the ceiling. "Maggie, you can find some greens almost anywhere, but it's here, in the pack, that you're guaranteed to find your fulfillment. Searching the stream's length on a whim for some trifle taste treat, you may never fatten up. Worse, you may be eaten up. You can't forsake producing eggs for your family," he reminded her. "You have to think about your contribution to them, to the stream, to the pack," he prodded. "You have to produce as many eggs as you can."

Maggie looked at the ground and said softly but decidedly, "I'm not ready for eggs yet! Anyway, am I necessarily better off spending all my time feeding and none of it looking for rich food? It takes good food, too, to produce many eggs."

"Yes, it does," Rudy replied, sounding a bit hurt by Maggie's suggestion that the pack's food wasn't good. "But beware of wasting your time looking for what you imagine to be perfect elsewhere. Heading out in the stream alone, far from the security of the pack, you risk no return."

"Isn't it also risky not to garner rich food because one fears the hazards of seeking it?"

"It's not fear I'm speaking of but responsibility," Rudy said emphatically. "Maggie, I have seen nymphs before—wandering, following their own minds, responsible only to themselves. I imagine that when they emerge, they zip around the other world engrossed in their new wings, flying high and forgetting the clan. What would happen to the stream if we all behaved so? I'll tell you: it would come undone if we all lived such license. The home we have here would decay if every nymph were allowed to pursue his or her own inclination."

Rudy shook his head, his palps pulled downward. He sighed deeply. "If you must ..." he said, and then he left her.

At dawn Maggie walked over the same terrain she had visited the day before. Aren't these rocks as good as any, she considered as she pulled a leaf off a small, fading cluster of yellow wedges of *meridion*. But the inner stream offered the possibility of richer patches. How could it hurt to spend a bit more time looking?

Maggie headed instream, daydreaming about good food, airy waters, and stable rocks. Gradually the terrain changed, and, imperceptibly, Maggie turned from daydreaming to foraging. Eating greens with the current running through her gills, standing on the firmness of rock, Maggie filled herself on what seemed her first decent meal in days.

Full, and ready to stretch her legs, Maggie decided to visit Rensaleer. Wanting to bring him something, she began to look for a grain of outstanding color or form. She looked into the crevices between rocks and into the dimples in the stones' surfaces; she looked among clumps of algae and under mats of moss. At first everything she saw looked the same, sand grains come to rest, but as she looked closer she began to recognize that some grains were the same and some were different. There were white grains with six faces and those with eight; there were faces that were fibrous and those that were smooth; there were smooth faces that were translucent and those that were opaque. Drawn in by the pleasure of recognition, Maggie wandered here and there, carrying around grains to compare.

The longer Maggie looked, though, the blurrier the distinctions among the grains became. It had been easier to see differences when she had looked only a little, for once she looked closer, the lines between what was this and what was that did not become more clear but more obscure.

Maggie finally settled on an irregularly rounded, translucent stone of indeterminable color. She had found it early in her search but wasn't sure of its distinctiveness. When she rotated the grain, its color changed from white to green to blue to violet. She didn't recall seeing any similar grains in Rensaleer's collection, so after one quick last look, she tucked the grain away and headed for the shallows.

Arriving at Rensaleer's lodgings, Maggie saw that his net was laden with foodstuffs and would very likely soon collapse from the weight. Thinking he must be gone on some collection trip, she pulled the larger pieces of clutter from the net. With Rensaleer's net thus rescued for the time being, Maggie went to see his collection, for she wanted to compare the grain she had brought.

The moment Maggie reached the foot of the path, she knew something was terribly wrong: loose threads waved in the current; a green grain lay atop a pile of purplish ones; a cylindrical red stone sat next to a pale-yellow plate. Maggie walked slowly along the wall in dismay, wondering what had happened to the orderly edifice. She spotted Rensaleer amid a tassel of unfastened threads and called to him.

Rensaleer turned and looked down at her. In a discouraged tone he said, "There was a wave in the pool with a new direction."

"Can you fix it?" asked Maggie.

"Ah-yup," replied Rensaleer, distracted.

Remembering the grain she had brought and thinking it might cheer him, Maggie brought forward her find. "Look what I found along the border of the inner stream."

Rensaleer crawled down the wall to look in her claw.

"Oh, opal," he said, reaching for the grain. His tone was already more cheerful. Maggie watched him rotate the grain slowly. "Opals are a lot like quartz," he told her, "but opals are amorphous. Have no internal structure." He held the grain out for Maggie to look.

"Are they rare?" Maggie asked.

Rensaleer nodded. "Relatively."

"Would you like it? I brought it for you."

"Oh, thank you. Will stick it right here for now," he said, tying the grain to an intact portion of the wall.

"Can I help?" asked Maggie.

"Not really." Rensaleer shook his head. "Just have to put everything back."

"Well, I guess I should leave you alone then ... my chatter would probably only distract you."

Rensaleer's silence affirmed her supposition.

"I'll come back later then," Maggie offered.

"Please do." Rensaleer said and forced a smile. He waved an antenna and returned his attention to the wall.

"Don't forget to eat," Maggie reminded him gently and then walked back up the path. She glanced at Rensaleer's net as she passed it but knew to unclog it for him would be useless; he wouldn't come to feed any time soon.

First over fine sand and then over coarser grains that stuck in her claws, Maggie walked instream. She passed lone hills and headed toward the range that extended into the stream's center. She was preoccupied with thoughts of Rensaleer's wall.

Rensaleer's collection made the sand he lived in, the sand she now walked over, seem comprehensible. She had begun to think that if one could determine the proper place of grains, one might be able to make some order out of the stream's seeming randomness. How reassuring a world of unambiguous entities would be. But one could not erect walls of threads and expect them to remain intact.

Instead of returning to the pack, Maggie spent the rest of the day along the margins of the inner stream eating, napping through the bright light, and watching what and who drifted by in the current. At dawn the next day, she returned to Rensaleer's.

Maggie found Rensaleer's collection more or less intact, but something about it was very different. There were still many gaps where Rensaleer had not yet replaced grains, but something more fundamental bothered her. Being so new to grain distinctions, Maggie was slow in recognizing what had changed.

Rensaleer noticed Maggie standing on the ledge and crawled across his collection to meet her. When he reached her side, she exclaimed, "These red cubes are next to white hexagons, and those pink octahedrons," she said excitedly, running down the wall, "are with orange ones! You've changed their places!"

"Yes," Rensaleer concurred, scurrying to catch up with her. "Before my final determination was based on color. Now thinking crystal shape might be more important."

"I thought the grains were arranged by a set of rules."

"Well, yes," Rensaleer replied as he retied a loose grain that dangled in front of them, "but what I know is continually changing."

"But if where a grain fits one day is not where it fits the next," asked a disconcerted Maggie, "how will you ever know if a grain is in its right place, which grains truly belong together?"

"Probably never will know that. Only can arrange them by what I can see," Rensaleer said, busily anchoring another grain. "And some placement is better than no placement."

Maggie raised a cloud of sand as she vented her gills in a deep breath of frustration. She had thought the order of the grains concrete even if the threads that held them together weren't. Rensaleer had arranged a place for everything, and as long as the stream had flowed smoothly, everything had remained in its place. Grains alike were placed together and grains unalike were placed apart. With Rensaleer's grains re-coordinated on the basis of his new viewing, whether a row went here or there now seemed somewhat arbitrary to Maggie.

Rensaleer climbed a few rows above Maggie's head to fasten down yet another grain. "How are things at the pack?" he called down.

"Well, everyone is very friendly ..." Maggie replied, "very thoughtful ... quite close, in fact."

"Sounds lovely," Rensaleer said, already occupied by two rows of translucent white crystals.

"I guess I should return—I've been gone since yesterday."

"Have you?" Rensaleer asked. Without waiting for an answer, he started to murmur, "Yes, striations on the cleavage face clearly in these specimens."

Seeing Rensaleer was already absorbed, Maggie called, "Take care, Rensaleer."

"Oh, yes, bye."

Maggie took a moment to look over the grandiose wall, which Rensaleer would construct over and over as need be, for he loved to decide what was this and what was that, to give names to grains and secure their place. It had been her mistake to think a wall of well-organized grains might help her find her way to the richest of foods. How could she forget that unforeseen currents could tumble even the greatest of boulders?

The soft clatter of grains tapping against one another held Maggie's attention. How they sparkled in the bright light of the shallows. Maggie looked for Rensaleer, but he had already been lost from her sight. One of those shiny yellow grains was actually Rensaleer's head, and his thin body was entwined with some connecting thread.

Maggie walked up the path and past Rensaleer's lodgings and food net, which clogged with litter instead of food. She hoped Rensaleer would come to eat before his net became the fortuitous meal of some passerby but doubted that he would.

~~~~~~

"There you are," Rudy said when he saw Maggie. She was in the masticators' chamber, at the last grate through which the processed leaves passed.

"I went to visit Rensaleer," she explained.

"You should let us know when you're going to be gone," Rudy admonished. "We depend on you being here ... and we were worried."

"Well, I—" Maggie stammered, feeling guilty about her transgression. "It was fortunate that I went," she added quickly to deflect Rudy's reproach. "Rensaleer's collection had just been taken apart by the current."

"Poor Rennie," Rudy said sympathetically and hooked his foreclaw on the grate. "He's worked so hard at putting that thing together."

"Well, he's already put it back together," Maggie said, shaking her head. "And do you know what? He's put it back together totally different."

"I'm not surprised," Rudy said. "Look at what he's working with: a bunch of grains. Rennie can tie those things
~~~~~~

down until his salivary glands run dry, but he can't keep them from getting knocked around by the currents. There's nothing that holds those grains together, except Rennie, and it takes a lot of work to maintain a coherent entity in a stream that's always ready to dismantle it." Rudy sighed and shook his head.

"That's why we have to teach our young the way of the pack." Rudy released the grate and turned to face the masticators. His palps spread in a smile. "The currents could reshuffle the stream tomorrow and pull apart this leaf jam, but we'd be ready to coalesce a new pack elsewhere. As individuals we couldn't do this, as individuals we'd be washed away in the drift with everyone else. But the pack gives us a solid foundation; it is our rock."

"Rensaleer sees his wall as his rock," Maggie observed.

"Yes," Rudy nodded sadly, "he does. That's why I doubt that he'll ever realize his fulfillment."

"He certainly doesn't nourish toward it," Maggie said, thinking of the gaping holes in Rensaleer's net. "I hope he reaches his adulthood with full wings with which to take his flight."

"I wouldn't mind him wingless if I could be sure he'd produce his young," Rudy said.

"Oh," said Maggie dreamily, "I wouldn't want to miss out on my wings."

"All that foraging for only wings! Nah!" Rudy scrunched his eyes and mouth together; the large teeth of his lower lip almost touched the base of his antennae. "More stoneflies are what I look toward," he said with zeal. "From the stream we will emerge; eggs will be laid upon the waters, and they will hatch; young nymphs will seek leaf packs, and there they will meet elders."

From the stream the stoneflies will emerge, thought Maggie, into a denselessness they have never known. Will some get dizzy, no longer hampered by their heavy bodies? She watched the young masticators. Encouraged by this sudden release, will some fly high and stray from the pack?

"And elders will teach young nymphs the way of the pack," Rudy described their future, "how the young nymphs should behave once the elders are gone. And when the elders emerge, the young nymphs will take their place and become the teachers, to repeat the cycle again."

No, few stoneflies will fly away. Maggie looked up at the leafy ceiling overhead. From the stream to the other world and back to the stream again, they will voyage without wonder. Eggs will be laid on the waters—

"Yes," Rudy beamed as he looked over the brood of masticators, "the more we put in, the more we get out!"

—to produce more stoneflies, Maggie thought.

"Together, we create an entity of new magnitude," Rudy rested his claw on Maggie's wing pad, "a magnitude less vulnerable, more secure. Together, we create an entity that is lasting."

Leaf fragments plastered into walls. Maggie looked around the chamber. Yes, this new entity has lain down its own integument, so it can remain an intact mass. Out of songs emerges a solid body whose inners work as one, everyone's role defined.

"And we have purpose here in the stream," Rudy reminded Maggie: "to take the old and used and return it to the stream as new and enriched."

Maggie began to fidget with some leaf fragments at her foreclaws. "Rudy," Maggie looked up, "if how we fit together becomes how we must fit together, isn't something lost? In the face of the freedom of denselessness, there are those who might fly high and forget the clan. But if we so fear this possibility that we deny the reward of flight, what does our foraging become?"

"Flight is just a brief moment," Rudy said. "Our real reward is foraging with the certainty that our efforts have meaning. If we want this fulfillment, we must maintain the home in which we can find it. Speaking of which," Rudy shook Maggie by her wing pad, "we both should return to our stations." With that said, he left.

Maggie turned around and faced the grate. It was planted in the downstream wall of the chamber and spanned most of the chamber's length. It was larger than any of the other grates in the pack, yet its mesh was the finest of all, for only small detritus was to pass through it. Maggie moved to a quiet corner and gingerly scraped from the mesh bacteria densely coated with fine leaf flakes.

Take away the old, make room for the new. In a ripening mass of leaves that insulated them from the rest of the stream, the stoneflies conducted their converting process. Take away the old, make room for the new—along pathways made inflexible, for the pack worked best when no minds wandered. Yes, for the stream they produced their morsels: much food, more food, the same food, over and over, without change. Suddenly, in the midst of this community, Maggie felt isolated, her penchant for algae denied. If she stayed with the pack, would her taste for algae fade, would dreams of her flight dim?

Maggie looked through the grate and into the darkness that she knew led outside. Somewhere in light and denselessness there was something that the algae captured in their synthesis that Maggie sought to touch in her flight. Leaf litter would always be replenished, but would the pack be rejuvenated without a breath of unhampered flight in the other world?

Maggie continued to scrape the grate quietly. Soon it was rectime. While the masticators left the chamber, Maggie remained at her post. The young stoneflies proudly passed this loyally efforting mayfly. But as soon as Maggie saw the last of the stoneflies exit, she dashed across the chamber, darted into a tunnel, and ran away from the reproach of one hundred pairs of stonefly eyes.

CHAPTER FIVE

TWISTED VINES AND TANGLED TENDRILS

The mountain range that formed the pack's dam extended far into the inner stream, so when Maggie left the leaf pack, she looked for a pass through the mountains near the stream's margin, for here the current would be gentler. She found a promising canyon between two low peaks.

Upon rounding a bend in the pass, Maggie stepped into a peculiar reach. Great, gnarled woody limbs rose from the muddy, brown ground. They arched overhead and wove around one another. Some branches returned to the mud whereas others disappeared from sight. Little light penetrated this dense labyrinth, even though it was close to the edge of the stream.

Maggie's brownness blended well with the ground here, so she started through the woods quickly, but after passing several twisted limbs she was stopped by a dense green web of water net that swayed in the gentle but persistent current. There was a strange feel to the water here: it seemed to flow in an unseen path beaten down to make a predictable course through an unpredictable terrain.

In the darkness and shadows of these knotted woods, Maggie could barely see ahead. Holding still on hardened mud, she discerned that just beyond where she stood was a dense forest of tangled vines.

Maggie had been warned about tendrils such as these: one could never be certain of what they harbored, and once in their midst, one might already be endangered. But the mysterious unknown held Maggie transfixed. She cautiously crept around the water net and a bit closer to the tendrils and then held still. Standing at the base of a heavy wooden trunk, she peered into the vines to see what within she was to fear.

A flicker of movement caught Maggie's attention. She looked downstream along a narrow furrow of open ground that ran through the dense tangle and eventually disappeared into the darkness of the vines. Again there was a movement. Behind a small rock mound in the furrow, a long, thin leg was raised into the water and then brought down. Maggie recognized the leg as that of a caddisfly and decided to go query the caddis on the locale.

Making her way cautiously along the edge of the furrow, Maggie approached the rock. She stopped beside a gnarled stump close to the caddisfly and called out a greeting but received no response. Wondering why the caddis was so ambivalent to her approach, Maggie stepped away from the stump and into the furrow. Now within the caddis's plain sight, she called to him again. Still, he did not answer. She took a few more steps toward him, and the caddisfly finally moved. But the movement was not his own; instead, a gentle wave created by Maggie's last steps had dislodged him. Although seemingly whole, the caddisfly was without livingness. His body rose from where it had been wedged, and the greater current took him away. Maggie's setae tingled. Reflexively, she lay low to the ground, motionless.

This was not the work of a fish or a dragonfly. No, with them one would disappear. In this tangle where all was shaded, all forms obscured, it had taken Maggie a long time to recognize lifelessness.

Maggie became angry with herself. Just because she had six legs, must she scurry in whatever direction was before her eyes? What should she do now? Still lying close to the ground, with only the slightest movement of her head, Maggie looked around to see how she might get out of this tangle. Darkness and denseness were everywhere—except just upstream of her. There, in the bank of tendrils that cloaked the edge of the stream, a small gap allowed some light into the dark grove. She crawled toward the light slowly, pausing at each step, hoping to attract no one's attention.

At the opening, Maggie warily peeked into a small inlet. Dense, twisted vines enclosed a bay in a brown and green curtain. An unobstructed column of light illuminated the center of this arena. Maggie's eyes rested on the few rocks there.

"And how long will you linger at the enn-trrance?" a voice asked. Maggie jumped backward into the furrow, and the unseen speaker laughed. Then disclosing herself from the wall of tendrils was a streamling unfamiliar to Maggie.

With a long, lean body of green, the water scorpion was barely distinguishable from the vines from which she hung upside down. Her body was at least three times as long as Maggie's and bobbed up and down in the current as if one of the tendrils. It was only the water scorpion's big black eyes that gave her location away.

"I—I—I'm not lingering," stuttered Maggie, intimidated by this cryptic creature.

"Well, then," laughed the water scorpion, "take a step in or out, for you are obscuring my view."

Although a bit offended by this streamling's bluntness, Maggie stepped in.

"Well now, welcome to Loveta's cove," said Loveta. Her mouth was a tapered beak, which she pulled to the side in what appeared to be a smirk.

"Lov-eat-ah's cove?" asked Maggie.

Her beak tucked in demurely, Loveta replied, "Yes. Loveta. Me. This is my place."

"Oh. Doesn't anyone else live here?"

"Of courrrse ..." Loveta said, extending her words as if to match the length of her limbs. "But no one is around right now—just me." Then she added flirtatiously, "And now you. Have you been in the neighborhood lllong?" Her beak was pulled back, making her big eyes look largely innocent.

"No, I've just arrived," Maggie told her. "I've never been in a jungle before. The woods and vines are so dense that it's impossible to see. That's what brought me to the entrance of your cove—it's clear of all the clutter."

"Ah, yes, the jungle is dense. And more eyes watch you than you might guess." Loveta clasped her tendril with her mid- and hindlegs and moved effortlessly up the vine backward. She stopped when the tip of her long, hollow tail touched the top of the stream. Having thus made herself comfortable, she offered, "You can rest here, in my cove. I have it very well guarded."

"So the jungle is a dangerous place," Maggie observed.

"It depends on who you are," replied Loveta.

"Well, I just saw a caddisfly whose body was whole but without livingness!" Maggie shuddered as she told Loveta.

"Oh my!" said Loveta in shocked surprise. "These waters have been very good to me, but one does need to know how to live in them. For example, I am seen only when I want to be." She demonstrated this by pulling herself to her vine and rapidly becoming part of it. If Maggie hadn't kept her eyes on those of Loveta, Loveta would have completely disappeared. Loveta then stretched her legs back out, returning to her sociable position.

"I don't think these waters would be very good to me," Maggie said. "In fact, I'd like to find a safe route out of them as soon as possible."

"Well perhaps I can help you with finding a route," Loveta offered. Her beak moved to the side and rested in a playful expression. "But for now, why don't you rest? You look tired." Clasping her tendril with her hindlegs, she floated forward. "Please, make yourself at home."

"I am tired," Maggie admitted, ruffling her gills. "I've had a full day, and these slow waters are wearing."

"Ah yes, you are a creature of flowing waters, rocks, greens—I do have some rocks," Loveta said sweetly, "and they do have some greens. Please go ahead and have something to eat if you'd like. I'm not a grazer."

Maggie had been standing on the silty ground just inside the entrance of the cove. She was hesitant about going to the rocks, where she would be encircled by vines in almost still waters. But the rocks and greens were alluring. She swam to the center of the cove.

"How well you swim," Loveta complimented her.

From the rocks Maggie could see Loveta more clearly. Loveta's face was small, which at a distance had been hidden by her very large, round eyes. In the narrow space between these eyes were her small antennae and her stout, beak-shaped mouth. The beak had three segments, each of which moved independently, accenting Loveta's words and translating them into a language unfamiliar to Maggie.

Close to Loveta's face sat her peculiar forelegs; the thin lower portion of these legs remained tightly folded against their stout bases. Her mid- and hindlegs were uniformly slender, and her hindlegs could have easily reached the tip of her grooved tail filaments, with which she siphoned air from the other world. Loveta had had her wings since her third molt, and they were folded snugly over her long, narrow back.

"I'm not much of a swimmer," Loveta confided, "but as you can see, there's little open water here in which to swim.

And I really don't need to move that often; I get all my food amongst these vines." She casually reached for another tendril and floated over to it, demonstrating the insignificance of her movements to Maggie.

As if at a stoneflies' convergence, Maggie said, "Perhaps we mayflies move around so much because our food is so spread out."

"Yes, perhaps ..." Loveta said slowly, her beak pulled aside in its seemingly mocking smile.

Moving effortlessly to another vine, Loveta slid down to the ground to allow for a more intimate exchange. "I don't often have mayfly visitors," she said sweetly. "I suppose these waters don't suit your kind. What brought you here?"

"Well, I've been looking for some good foraging grounds," Maggie answered, "but now I wonder if I should have stayed where I was, for in my hopeful wandering I've managed to come to this perilous terrain." Then, remembering what Loveta had said earlier, Maggie reminded her, "You said you might be able to help me find a way out?"

"Yes," Loveta replied. "But won't you please stay awhile—eat, rest, and keep me company."

Actually, Maggie wanted to depart as soon as possible. Although Loveta's words were inviting her to stay, Loveta's beak seemed to be taunting her.

Maggie glanced down at the available forage. A few fat diamond-shaped *frustrulias* lay side by side in a gelatinous spread, and fatter *surirellas* were scattered about. She then spied some reasonably sized *achnanthes* and gratefully bit into the small cluster. While she chewed a second mouthful, she felt Loveta's big eyes watching her. Perhaps Loveta really did want some company; her cove certainly was a quiet place.

Loveta migrated back up her vine and remarked, "I had a big meal just awhile ago. I often like to sleep after I eat. Do you?" Her beak was tucked back, making her big eyes even more prominent.

"Yes, after a big meal, in a safe crevice."

Loveta clasped an adjoining vine and released the one she had been holding. "Have you ever met anyone in my family before?"

"No."

"I guess that's because you've never been in these waters. There are a number of us here."

"Oh," Maggie said, a bit surprised. "It must be nice to have relations about to visit."

"Oh, we don't visit much. We're all solitary sorts; we make one another a bit jittery."

"I just spent a few days with a clan of stoneflies. They enjoyed one another's constant company."

"A clan of stoneflies." Loveta's legs floated toward a nearby vine. "That would be a lot of ... fun."

"It was for a while. We sang together, swam together, danced together, ate together. But then we were supposed to, well, think together, and I guess it's a bit hard to think like a stonefly if one is a mayfly. ..." Maggie became lost in her thoughts.

"And how do mayflies think?" Loveta's voice startled Maggie. Loveta had moved across several vines, and Maggie had to turn to see her.

"I'm not sure," Maggie said. "The stoneflies believed they would find all they could ever want in their pack. Perhaps I, too, am a solitary sort. There is a place I've been looking for—I thought I might find something like it with the stoneflies, but then I realized I wouldn't."

"Never is the best shared," Loveta observed.

"I don't know," Maggie said. "Perhaps somewhere there is something good and plentiful enough for all of us to share."

"Perhaps somewhere," Loveta said with dismissal, "but one must never forget to take care of oneself. In the jungle, in the waters of the stream, those who don't are soon fish food."

"One needs to be cautious," Maggie nodded in agreement.

"One needs always to watch, for there is always someone who will try to take one's cove." Loveta's beak was not pulled into its usual smirk but was thrust forward. She spoke of matters not to be mocked.

"I guess that's a problem with having a cove," Maggie said, backing up to the far end of the rock.

"And without a cove, who would I be?" Loveta said, her beak extended forward. "I'd be a wandering piece of fish food." She laughed, and then, with a not yet displayed briskness, she moved across several vines in rapid succession. The brown and green curtain quivered in her wake. "Here, I decide who visits and how long they may stay. Plllease," her tone suddenly became gentle again, "have some more to eat."

Maggie looked at Loveta's face; she wasn't sure if she should be flattered at being an invited guest. Unconsciously, she took another step back and found herself teetering on the edge of the rock, so she propelled herself sideways to a nearby stone. Landing smoothly, she thought of her own fast waters, where holding one's own ground was often difficult enough, let alone claiming a cove. She gently plucked an *achnanthes* from the stone and remarked, "The current is so slow here, but it is very persistent."

Loveta slid down her vine. "Yes, little change comes to these waters. At times, though, there's a change in whom sits where."

"In my waters," Maggie observed, "the stream at times rearranges where we all sit."

"But it always provides for some to sit on top," Loveta said quickly but coolly, her beak sitting between smirk and seriousness. "Others may get tossed around, but I don't."

"Even in floods?"

"Floods don't wash away the depths of the jungle, for the path of the current is deeply engrained." Loveta glided a few vines closer to Maggie and pulled aside some tendrils to reveal a dark passageway. "And I have caves—caves in which I can cling tightly to deeply rooted vines." With her beak pulled back, her eyes large in feigned innocence, Loveta asked sweetly, "Would you care to see them?"

Maggie looked into the darkness and shook her head no.

"No, I didn't think you'd want to see the caves." Loveta let the curtain of tendrils fall back into place. "The waters there are quite still, but you'd see the stream for itself instead of for its passing." Loveta went back up her vine and pierced the top of the stream with her tail to draw her breath.

"But there's no light from the other world in your caves," Maggie said as she looked up at Loveta in the dimming light of the cove; "in that they're very different from the rest of the stream."

"The light of the other world!" Loveta laughed. "Do you really believe the other world will be any different from here?"

"In the other world there is denselessness," Maggie asserted defensively. "Waters won't tumble us about as they do in the stream. And in the other world we shall fly! We won't use our legs to carry us about as we do here but our wings. There we shall move with a freedom we have never known."

"You think denselessness will offer you freedom?" Loveta said curtly, her beak thrust forward. She grabbed another tendril and hung between two vines. "You don't see where you are, do you? Do you think freedom is some ability to fly about? Do you think the rules of the other world are any different from those of the stream?"

Loveta's beak suddenly relaxed. She gently moved to another vine and said in a soft tone, "Not very long from now I shall begin to spend my nights in the other world, my days here. With my adulthood imminent, I have had to face that while I am gone transients, likely another water scorpion, will come to my cove. They will think that they can take it for their own. Each day when I return, I shall have to tell these transgressors to leave, that I shall not be usurped, that this is my perch. The freedom of denselessness is insubstantial. It is those who hold power who have freedom. That, my dear mayfly, is, has been, and will always be the rule."

"But then most of us shall never have any freedom," Maggie pointed out.

"Well, if some of us are to be on top, then some of us have to be beneath." Loveta slid to another vine. "And it's very clear where we each stand."

Well it was becoming very clear to Maggie where she stood: on a small rock with no crevice, in slow waters with no safe terrain, and with a water scorpion whose hospitality was seeming ever more less generous—a bad spot to be in.

Suddenly, Loveta stretched herself across the entrance of the cove, making it quite clear where she stood. "One is just another piece of fish food," she said, thrusting her beak forward, "unless one takes control." And then for the first time she unfolded her peculiar forelegs and, with a "snap," their thin blades sprung back instantly to their tightly tucked hold.

"We all can be fish food," Maggie said, her eyes on Loveta's forelegs as she backed up to the far edge of her small refuge.

"Uhm, yes, there is that possibility," Loveta said as if bored by the wasted words, "but here I have the power of the fish." She then jerked the vines she held, causing a ripple to course around the arena.

Frightened by the shadow of movement that ran around her, Maggie jumped off the rock. She scurried beside her bulwark, wanting to remain hidden but with Loveta in her view. Maggie peered out from the corner of the rock and called, "What if we all had the power of the fish? What, then, would the stream become? There must be a way to allow those who don't seek such power to persist."

Loveta looked straight at her. "Certainly! It always pays to keep a stock of your type around. It makes life a lot ... fuller." She started laughing.

"See! Your power is good only if you're one of the few who has it."

"So?" Loveta ridiculed Maggie and then dangled forward toward her.

Maggie ran behind the rock. In her haste, she tripped over an empty caddisfly case. Images of the dead caddis flooded her mind. Holding her prey fiercely, tenaciously, Loveta had pierced the caddis's skin with the tip of her beak and had taken his life fluid. Once the caddis's livingness was gone, she had thrown his empty body into the current, for there was nothing left to be had. Except power. Power to take life. Power to decide fate. That is what made her strong. Yet even as she was assimilating the caddisfly's life fluid, she felt her power dissipate, and she hungered for it again.

"Couldn't we respect one another's integrity?" Maggie suggested as she peeked over the top of the rock.

Loveta laughed at her. "You have to claim your integrity." Then Loveta flexed her forelegs and pulled the vines toward herself, narrowing the entrance of the cove.

"So you respect only those who have your strength?" Maggie tried pushing against Loveta's blockade.

"And how should I look upon those without strength, with compassion? Compassion gets eaten in a stream where it isn't shared. Ha! Shield yourself with your compassion!" Loveta lunged toward Maggie. Just beyond Loveta's grasp, Maggie jumped back and scrambled farther behind the rock.

Loveta retracted, laughing. "How can you expect me to take you seriously?"

Maggie's setae were tingling; her joints ached from her fright. So far she had amused Loveta, but soon Loveta would strike. Loveta had held her captive with taunts and surety. With each imperceptible move from one vine to the next, Loveta had left a shadow for Maggie to spar.

It was late in the day, and the back of the arena lay in semidarkness. Maggie retreated to a rock there.

"Your attitude will bring the stream the least it can be!" Maggie protested from behind the rock.

"Look around you," Loveta instructed as she rotated her head in a circle. "The stream works, and the way it works is readily apparent."

Maggie looked around herself: Loveta barred the entrance of the cove; the rock was, at best, temporary shelter; and around her was the darkening curtain of twisted vines. "Is what we readily see the only way the stream can be?"

"It's the only way we need to know," Loveta denied her.

"The direction of the stream is and won't change," Maggie said, "but the currents that bring me here, bring another there—these things of the currents are circumstance." Trusting that the only one to fear in the cove was Loveta, Maggie ran across the open ground and into the shadow of the tendrils.

Loveta dropped down the vine and looked straight at Maggie. "And circumstance," Loveta smiled smugly, "is all that matters here. When we meet, I win. Your fate is decided, and my circumstance is perpetuated."

The thick vines pushed against Maggie, claiming their space. "Yes, your way seems forever perpetuated." Maggie took a few wobbly steps through the vines toward Loveta. "You look around and see evidence that confirms the world as you would have it. But your order is well guarded to deny change. In the long run, the survival of the fiercest will not yield the fittest stream."

"A mayfly speaks to me of the long run?" Loveta laughed.

Maggie continued unsteadily through the vines, which grabbed at her tail. "Should the way of the stream be determined by those who see its fewest possibilities?"

"Should we guide our lives by illusions that have no promise of fruition?" Loveta snapped. "One cannot fill one's belly on belief."

"But with belief, can't visions be brought forth, nurtured until they are strong enough to express themselves—to grow into their ideals."

"Ideals!" Loveta spat out the word. "Ideals are for fish food, to keep them moving until their day comes." She shot up the vine to get a breath of air.

Maggie didn't hesitate. She darted forward, through the vines and under Loveta's dangling body. Without pause she threw herself out of the cove and into the jungle's persistent current.

CHAPTER SIX

BY THE MOON'S LIGHT

There is no constant rhythm to the waters of the stream. It changes with the seasons, with the shape of rocks. Yet a rhythm is always there, even in silence—cushioning, gently reassuring that one is in the stream.

Having thrown herself into the current at the entrance of Loveta's cove, Maggie found that the persistent but gentle flow soon became a swift drag. She was pulled along the treeless furrow with all sorts of debris until the drag met a sharp bend in the edge of the stream. There, all was dispersed in several directions, and Maggie had the misfortune of being thrust upward. She was deposited on her back at the top of the stream, where a surface eddy immediately pulled her in. Petrified at being so exposed, Maggie flailed her legs about, trying to submerge herself. But her unsuccessful efforts resulted only in fatigue. She was caught in the surface tension of the boundary and could not overcome its strength.

Now she was lying still, her body carried in large circles by the water. Her antennae swayed back and forth, every bristle bent, as the eddy moved her immobility. Being half in the stream, half in the other world, Maggie realized how secure the water felt. The stream had body while the other world had none. In the denselessness of the other world, her legs traveled through nothingness.

Yet the world of air was alive. In the darkness, murmurs floated by—and scents, all sorts of scents. Every so often, an almost imperceptible current would pass and deposit a light sediment over her body. Eventually tasting a soft grain that had fallen on her palp, Maggie found it to be quite sweet. So there is food in the other world, she thought.

Lying between water and air, Maggie listened to the sounds of the stream: the sound of water as it rubbed rocks and mingled with the edge, as it pushed against her own body. And here, at the boundary, she heard a sound she could not yet have heard: the sound of water touching itself in the denselessness of the other world. These were sounds she had missed while in their midst, which seemed to belong only to parting.

By the time night light appeared and highlighted Maggie's outline at the stream's surface, Maggie was calm, even though at any moment she might be plucked from below by a fish. And from above—she hadn't given it thought before, but most likely there was some fish-like creature of the other world. Yet experiencing the strange weightlessness on her belly and looking down into the stream as opposed to up from its bottom were so curious that Maggie's thoughts were not of predators. Feeling the water as if for the first time, hearing it, brought her calm. She had been surrounded by the stream's waters her entire life, and although she would eventually leave them to live in the world of air, the stream was the only world she had yet known. In the stream's surroundingness, it had been easy to forget its being, to forget that it brings and takes and holds all. And now the stream, which was always there for the living, was her comfort in the face of a probable end. Although she dreamed of flying through denselessness, the stream was now where all her hope lay. How strange that the other world told her this.

Just as Maggie was thinking of the goodness of the stream, even with every bristle bent, she could feel it: the waves of a body approaching. A large body. And there was nothing she could do—not swim, not hide, not freeze. She was exposed at the boundary of the stream, and as Loveta had told her, she was powerless against the approaching beast. With the lymph racing through her, she waited while an eternity passed. The waves of the body began to engulf her. And then it came.

The most reassuring of voices cautioned, "The boundary is really no place for a soft skin like you."

From her upside-down vantage point, Maggie had a blurry view of a large, dark body.

"You're offering yourself for easy picking," the voice continued.

"I was caught in a current that left me here," Maggie explained to the body that apparently wasn't going to consume her.

"Well, one hopes you wouldn't perpetrate the situation," he said.

Maggie, compelled to be truthful, replied, "Well, actually, I threw myself into the drift." She was embarrassed at admitting this, for the stranger would likely conclude that she didn't realize the gravity of her situation.

Her admission, though, piqued the other's curiosity. He clasped his foreclaws together, pivoted on his last abdominal segment, and asked, "What is your name?"

"Maggie."

"Well hello, Maggie. I am Jacob," he said quite cheerfully. "If you don't mind the telling, why did you throw yourself into the current?"

"I don't mind telling you, but I really would like to get down from here."

"Hmm, so you don't find the boundary appealing?" he asked.

"Actually, it is rather extraordinary to touch the other world. It's so different from the stream—it seems to have no body to its being, yet it's very much alive."

"Ah, yes it is," Jacob said enthusiastically, happy to share the boundary experience. He commenced swimming in circles around Maggie, causing her to spin. "I wish all streamlings would come up here for the view before their emergence."

"But it is also rather frightening," Maggie hastened to remind him of her predicament.

"Oh yes," Jacob said and stopped swimming. Maggie's spinning slowed. "The boundary can be frightening. ... Let's see, how shall we get you down?"

"If you could just turn me right side up."

"That will be, in fact, a bit difficult. The boundary is quite adept at immobilizing one. Well, let's try." Jacob swam to Maggie's side and with his long forelegs tried to pull her down into the stream from above. When this didn't work, he tried to flip her over from below, but he couldn't break the surface tension. After gyrating a few moments in thought, he dived below the surface and tugged at her long tail filaments. Her body moved toward him. He tugged harder.

"Ow!" Maggie cried. "You're going to break my tail off!"

"Hmm," Jacob reflected as he returned to the surface. "Maggie, my apologies beforehand. I'm going to have to exert a little force here. Brace yourself."

Jacob left Maggie and swam to the margin of the stream. Finding a log, he pulled himself onto its rough surface and climbed into the other world. Above the water, he opened his rigid outer wings, unfolded his pliable flying wings, and entered the world of air. He flew high above Maggie and watched her for a moment as the eddy carried her in its endless circling. He then flew straight toward Maggie, and just before he reached her, he deftly folded his flying wings beneath his hard ones and extended his forelegs forward. As he crashed through the boundary, he grabbed Maggie's side with his foreclaws and pulled her with him as he dove toward the streambed. When her back hit his back, he released his grip.

Jacob touched the ground and then sprang back to the boundary. Maggie, being quite disoriented, floated where she had been left. Immediately the current began to pull her away. She quickly dove to the ground.

Looking up from the sheath of leaves on which she had landed, Maggie saw hovering over her a flat, ovoid body with hard, shiny, blackish skin. She had been rescued by one of the great four-eyed whirligig beetles, viewers of the denselessness above and the stream below. Although dwellers of the boundary, they, as Jacob had demonstrated, could fly into the world of air while still being able to dive into the stream. But mostly they remained at the interface of the two worlds, where they could view both.

Jacob's appearance was neat and trim, every fold held firmly in place. Maggie could see his stream-gazing eyes, but the pair that gazed into the other world was on the upper side of his head. Between his two sets of eyes were his antennae. Each had a large cupped flap at its base with which Jacob listened to boundary vibrations. His mouth was small and sat at the front of his short, flat-fronted head. He paddled the waters with flat mid- and hindlegs that were broad and triangular; his forelegs were slender.

"Thank you very much," Maggie said. "I don't think I would have lasted up there much longer."

"Are you all right?" Jacob asked.

"Yes. I'm feeling dizzy though—I guess from having what is up and what is down turned around."

"Disequilibrating, I'd imagine."

"And I think I began to dry out some."

"Ah, possibly," Jacob agreed. "My hard wings shield my back from the dryness of the world of air."

Breaking their stillness, Maggie climbed over a pile of leaves and onto a more comfortable log, where she ventilated her gills in the somewhat turbid waters. As Maggie relaxed so did Jacob. He returned to the habitual circling of the whirligig beetles. With his paddle-like legs he glided backward, forward, then round and round in small circles.

"The other world, the world of air," Maggie said, "it is so strange. Its dryness, its nobodiedness..." she reflected. "Things floated by—I could sense them."

"Ah yes," Jacob inhaled the thought. "Those qualities of the world of air that give buoyancy to livingness, that readily elude consciousness—so buoyant, with ease they escape the stream if they do not find a comfortable home, and they aren't guaranteed to stay even if they do. Those essences, ethereal clouds, whispers that permeate the denselessness. ..."

"You know these?" Maggie asked enviously, taken by his words.

Jacob looked at Maggie, all four eyes directed toward her, although she could not see this. "You may think me lucky to see into both the stream and the world or air, but for me it is torment as well as fortune. I have just a taste of the world of air: I experience its wonders, but with my body, heavy and clumsy, I cannot soar forever into its denselessness." His forelegs reached upward. "And likewise, although I can dive under the water and feel what it is like to be completely immersed, the air under my wings returns me to the boundary. Living here at the boundary of two worlds, I never live fully in either." His forelegs floated down.

"No," he continued, paddling backward, folding his slender forelegs to his body, "I must remain here, feeding on the remnants of sky and stream. My heavy, clumsy body says it is so. But without body, there is no substrate for the experience, no consciousness of the essences. Without body there would be no eyes from which to see." And this he said with sadness.

Jacob ceased paddling and was carried in a circle of the surface current. Maggie, wanting to hear more, began to follow after him but immediately became bogged down in the viscous mud that underlay her leafy island. She flurried her gills as she struggled to free herself from the mire.

"Oh, please forgive my rudeness," Jacob called and then rushed to her in a swift dive. Although Jacob appeared flat at the top of the stream, Maggie could now see that he was quite deep from back to belly. "Allow me to offer my assistance," he said. "I can guide you back to your own waters."

"I would appreciate that," Maggie replied a bit tersely as she freed the last of her legs from the mud.

Jacob darted back to the boundary. "This way," he said and began to direct Maggie through the mud along a path of leaves and logs. She followed her beacon.

"I apologize for so many words," Jacob said, paddling backward so that he could face Maggie. Then clasping his foreclaws together he laughed at himself and said, "Yes, yes, the words, the crux of the matter. You see, we whirligigs look from one world to the other, and betwixt them we try to explain, to join across the boundary. We try to bring from one world to the other that which does not readily cross, and we do so with the word."

"You communicate across the boundary," Maggie prompted the suddenly silent oval body above her, "so that we all might understand." Maggie had heard stories about the great whirligig beetles and was anxious to hear more.

"Yes, that is the form of what we do." He stroked the viscosity of the night's waters with alternating legs, and his pace slowed. Bringing his foreclaws to his mouth, he created a funnel and heralded, "My clan, the seekers of knowledge, the keepers of the pursuit"; then he let his funnel collapse. "I grew up believing and anxiously joined the school. To look into, to touch the world of denselessness, to touch and see that which is there that cannot be held, to touch this place. ..." His forelegs stretched out, reaching.

Jacob's longing resonated somewhere deep within Maggie.

"It was here that I lost my brethren," he said.

Maggie wondered how Jacob could lose anyone with so many eyes. It had not yet occurred to her that he was alone. The whirligig beetles typically traveled in great schools, busily exchanging communications about surface stimuli. "And where are your brethren?" Maggie asked.

"My brethren ..." Jacob trailed off in thought. Distracted from his paddling, he began to reel from side to side. He pressed his broad-tipped palps together; his eyes were focused on some place far away. "The faces of my brethren were once so familiar. I recognized them from my birth and aspired to join their ranks. But now the faces of my brethren are not so well-defined, and it becomes longer and longer between the seeing."

Jacob returned his water eyes to the stream and checked the path ahead. "It has been a long time since I have dwelt with my brethren. It became clear to them, and to me, that I no longer belonged."

"What happened?" Maggie asked. She climbed onto a log that reached high into the waters and followed one branch that brought her closer to Jacob. From high on the limb the waters seemed somewhat cleared of their silt, and the night light was brighter. Jacob's words seemed to float in the waters above her head, but his words were of things she wanted to know.

As if reenergized by Maggie's interest, Jacob began to swim backward in wide circles: a pass to the right of Maggie, through a point above her, and then a pass to her left. He began to hum a little tune to himself and became rather jovial.

"The word!" said Jacob. "I realized the imperfection of the word! And furthermore, I suggested," he mocked but then became serious, "that communication across the boundary is much more common than supposed; essences aren't conveyed only by the word but sometimes make their own way across." He swept his forelegs in an arc to demonstrate the ease with which things unembodied might move. "They leak through—I've felt their vibrations. And for my suggestion, I was ostracized."

"Why?" Maggie was puzzled. "I thought the whirligig beetles are the pursuers of knowledge, understanding?"

Fully recharged by Maggie's questioning, Jacob said boldly, "My suggestion had the potential of undermining our school."

"But the seekers of knowledge must look at all possibilities, mustn't they?"

"Ah, you speak of the ideal." Jacob caught her thought and whirled around her in long strides. "But the ideal is evasive, remaining afloat in the other world. Here, we each want to have the word. Enthusiasm for understanding soon gives way to enthusiasm for the self." Jacob stopped in front of Maggie. "My brethren want to be *the* communicators of the boundary, *the* keepers of the word. They want to be the only ones who can speak of both worlds."

The setae-fringed cups of Jacob's antennae twitched, and he quickly turned to his right. The cups twitched again, and

Jacob abruptly swam away in a zigzag. Maggie watched him disappear.

A wave heavy with sediment washed over her; detoured currents were continuously resuspending loose debris. Maggie looked down from her high perch at the ground around her. The night light lit the ground close by, but the landscape quickly faded into darkness. She could see only more of what she had been traversing—a mud lagoon with leafy islands and occasional log bridges. Just as she was beginning to wonder if Jacob would return to lead her the rest of the way, he reappeared, seemingly instantaneously.

"Just an aged leaf morsel," he said. "Shall we continue?"

Maggie descended the log and resumed following Jacob.

"If it is only your brethren who have the eyes to look into both worlds," Maggie asked, "aren't they the only ones who can speak of both?"

"We each have our senses with which to look into the world." Jacob dived into the waters and swam a broad circle around Maggie. He came alongside her and slowed his paddling. Each stroke of his legs created a wave that rolled over her, pressing her gills to her side. He looked at her with his upper eyes while his lower eyes skimmed the ground directly beneath him.

"So ready are we to say what we see, yet none of us has the gift to see all," he said. "To give form to the seeing—a thought crystallized, its rays permeating the waters with clarity," his words flowed out. "Articulation can be the liberation of comprehension." He suddenly sped ahead to view the terrain and then, as quickly, returned.

"But the word, language, is so very tricky," he continued as he swam and Maggie walked. "We name to distinguish, to set apart, but in describing we make the presumption of knowing, in defining the mistake of confining. Words," his forelegs glided forward from his mouth, "give the illusion of grasping that which is ethereal, so we are free to go on to something else with the idea packaged neatly away. The idea packaged neatly away!" He shook clenched foreclaws in exasperation. "As if an entire complexity can be simplified to one word!" Jacob darted to the boundary and swam in small, tight circles.

They moved on in silence for a while. A waft of airy water ran across Maggie's face. She was left somewhat disheartened by Jacob's words, but she also was left somewhat reassured— reassured because she had met someone who knew qualities that were not apparent but permeated the waters in which she lived and filled the denselessness she hoped to fly. Still, she did not know if she would find these essences, and it was not clear that anyone could show them to her.

"To perpetuate our myth, one is bestowed with the fruit garnered," Jacob said softly. "And not to … one is kept without place, searching the harder for each morsel." He waved his foreleg in front of his stream-gazing eyes to brush away the thought.

Jacob rode the surface silently; his broad legs cut forward through the water and then pushed back against it. The current was picking up.

This was not what Maggie had expected to hear about the school of the great truth seekers. But it was happily that she stepped onto her first rock, albeit it was a small one. She and

Jacob had finally reached the main channel of the stream, and the ground was littered with pebbles. Maggie took a few steps on this first stone and then sprang to another and then another. Upon landing on the third, she dislodged a small *microthamnion* bush. She watched the little shrub float away; it rose upward as it was pulled gently downstream. Then she saw Jacob's sharply defined outline move toward it: a line forward; a shorter one back; a half circle to the right; a short zigzag forward; a small tight circle around the bush; a tug at one branch; the plant eaten; a backward loop returning to her.

Revitalized, Jacob said cheerfully, "You were to tell me the story of your recent disengagement."

"Oh. Yes." Maggie recalled it reluctantly. She jumped to another stone. "Well, not far upstream I came upon the jungle of a strange streamling. I should have quit when I arrived, but at first I saw no threat." Maggie hesitated but then admitted, "And Loveta, a water scorpion, was mesmerizing. She seemed everything I am not—powerful, decisive. But then she began to taunt me. She challenged me to pit my strength against hers. She laughed at me and called me fish food." Maggie looked at the ground. "I threw myself into the drift to escape."

"At times we affirm what we are by saying what we are not," Jacob pointed out.

"But I ran away."

"Wasn't that the only path to perseverance?"

"Yes, for fish food," Maggie said with discontentment. "I can't keep running away from things I don't like."

"Perhaps the difference," Jacob suggested, a foreclaw pressed to his palps, "is between the 'running away from' and 'leaving for.' Might it not be a matter of who effected the walk?"

Maggie crossed a pale pink pebble. "Well, I'm sure Loveta would say it was she who effected my walk because I'm too powerless to affect anything."

"Dear Maggie," Jacob gently prodded as his body rocked in a ripple at the surface, "if you are so in doubt as to where you might, should, or do stand, readily others will make their suggestions—some in ready kindness, others in ready selfishness. Should your movements be guided by someone who wishes only to gobble you up? The water scorpion measured and assigned you according to her interests—why try to measure up to her values?"

"She said the things I value are worthless."

"Should you give her your own doubts with which to consume you?"

Jacob paddled ahead, and when he returned, he bent their course slightly downstream, so they wouldn't have to cut across the now stronger current.

"There are arguments you'll never be able to win with such as a water scorpion, but that doesn't mean you're wrong," Jacob reassured Maggie as he paddled steadily. "You can't change the way the water scorpion sees the world, but should you change to be who she wants you to be?" He pulled his antennae together in concentration. "So often there is coercion to settle for less than what we want, for others feel our doing so will give them more. But in the end, don't we all have more if each of us has more?"

"Loveta certainly wouldn't agree to that," Maggie answered for the lean water scorpion. "And she certainly sees no value in something that cannot be made concrete to show her."

"Ah, the water scorpion, with such large eyes, one might think her vision broad." Jacob glided out of Maggie's sight.

The night light was high in its cycle now, and the waters glimmered in its glow. The pebbles Maggie had been hopping between had become larger, and between them fine sand had replaced the mud. The water was crisp, now cleared of silty sediment.

Away from twisted vines and among hard-surfaced stones, Loveta and her laws were losing their grip on Maggie, as if Loveta's power was eroded by the stream's full current. As opposed to Loveta's arena, where ideas persisted among well-worn pathways, here things without form persisted by their resilience in the flow.

Maggie didn't know the laws the stream abided by—it was hard to see the stream through itself. Yet she still wondered if there were any truths, concrete or ethereal, she could come to know. "Jacob," she called, "will I ever come to know the nature of the stream?"

"We look, and with looking we see many things," Jacob responded, reemerging from the darkness. "But without already knowing, how can we ever be certain? Many readily claim the vision." Jacob's antennal cups twitched, and he began to dart off reflexively, but he quelled the impulse and returned. "There is not one word but many—and they all may say something of the nature of our stream.

"That is why I seek a community," he told Maggie, "a community in which I can listen to others, letting their eyes and words tell me ways I know not, so I can see more; a community in which the greatest wisdom and least ego is called for—that is what I seek."

"Really?" Maggie asked, hopeful at the prospect. "Where is this place?"

"Somewhere, I've heard," he said. "Somewhere, it is supposed to be."

"And are you going there?"

"I am looking." He circled unconsciously. "I've been looking." His paddling slowed, his thoughts in a place far off. "If only I could fly into that cloud, that whisper—to be bodiless amongst the essences. ... But this body, these words—these words are such a habit I don't know if I could stop them even for a moment." Jacob's eyes looked not at Maggie but to the other world. "Those nebulous clouds of essence I force into words, trying to bring them into the stream, so we can see their form. I almost kill them doing so, for their nature is transmuted, making them only remnants of what they were. Yet now easier I taste the words than those things that give them their meaning."

Jacob let his words be carried away by the waters, not wanting to hold on to them. He brought himself back to the stream and watched Maggie as she crossed a wide strip of coarse grains that filled a gap between larger rocks. Her footing was unsure on the tiny pebbles that provided, at most, room for one claw. Once she had firm footing on a larger rock Jacob asked, "What brought you to the jungle of the piercer, Maggie?"

His question asked her something she could scantly remember. She tried to focus on an answer, but she didn't know where to start. What had brought her here? The currents. She could have passed along another route, and Jacob never would have rescued her. How strange one's life becomes arranged at any given moment. A loose thread adrift in the current is held. Threads rearrange, and, perhaps even immediately, another is unfastened. When and where a loose thread connects can be a thousand different places, yet only a thousand, for threads are delicate and cannot fasten just anywhere. In asking herself how else the threads could have become arranged, the answer seemed explained to Maggie. But the why, the what? Hoping an explanation would make sense once she started, she began.

"Since the day I was washed from my first pool—" she said and then stopped. No, she thought, that's not quite it. Let's see, it was my last pool. ... But before she told Jacob this, she stopped again and thought, no, that's not it either.

"I've been looking for the patches that will bring me the most," she said.

"The most what?" Jacob asked with curiosity.

"Well, like everyone, I want rich eggs, and for them, I need the richest of foods."

Jacob stroked the water silently.

"So I've decided to move from reach to reach to gleam the richest of what is there. Not every reach will be rich," Maggie explained, "but there should always be a few bright spots. Perhaps sometimes I'll find reaches that are full of nothing but the richest sustenance." She turned her foreclaws up to suggest her possible good fortune, but when she remembered her recent misfortune, she returned her claws to the ground. "I realize I shall never know what lies ahead, that I'll increase my chances of being taken by a fish, but at least I'll have the chance to find the best, if I am willing to take the chance to look." A full, steady current lifted her gills from her sides.

"And in the end you will be richer?" Jacob asked, swimming tighter circles in the stronger current.

"I don't know," Maggie admitted. "Sometimes I think I miss what there really is to be had. I see others growing fatter, more robust, more content. Sometimes I think I'm just too impatient, and I fear my discontentment, for it takes me on a risky path. But Jacob, it's not just the pabulum that makes my body grow whose nourishment I seek. No matter how much I eat there is still a hunger, a hunger that tells me it's not enough to be fat to leave the richest of eggs. I will not feed in the other world, so brief will be my life there. Perhaps that is why I long to find a patch where the richness of the other world has entered the stream—so I can feel it, taste it, feed on it while I am here. And so I keep looking for that patch—a patch that has a quality that is not diminished by the taking, that is forever rejuvenated, forever replenished; a patch that will fill me and give me a special richness for my eggs. That is what I seek to find." And that was all she could say because she didn't know what else to call this place.

Jacob's eyes were full of longing. "Your hunger is still here, Maggie, isn't it?" he asked, a note of sadness in his voice.

"Yes."

"So you must go and fill it," he encouraged her.

"And you?"

"I shall return to the eddies. I cannot well navigate the surface of fast waters. And at the margin I can better feel my morsels in the surface tension."

Wanting to stay but wanting to look, hungry, fatigued from her night's journey, Maggie knew she should take her leave.

"Thank you, Jacob, for saving me."

Jacob circled her and replied, "Thank you, Maggie, for your company."

With this, Maggie took a few steps instream through the well-aired waters. Yet there was still something she wanted to know.

"The community, Jacob, how will you find it?"

"I don't know, Maggie. It has been long since I have tasted it."

But in the water between them was something they both tasted; it permeated Maggie's skin quickly and deeply. Maggie believed the place of which Jacob spoke could be found, but she didn't know if Jacob believed any longer that it could be. Jacob was a creature of the boundary, and from her limited experience, Maggie knew the boundary brought a strange admixture of calm and fear. And Jacob, perpetually straddling both, lived his fear in calm, and with time, his calm in fear.

Searching for words, she called, "Jacob."

A smile spread across his palps, and he called cheerfully, "Goodbye Maggie, the may fly." And then Jacob, the lone whirligig beetle, swiftly returned to gracefully gliding the boundary, navigating his path amongst life's imperfections.

CHAPTER SEVEN

OF CADDISFLIES, MILFOILS, AND CURRENTS

After parting with Jacob at the inner stream's margin, Maggie looked forward to a reach of steady flowing waters over broad plateaus. Instead, while the current became steady, the terrain of rock islands interspersed with coarse grains gradually became one of rock islands interspersed with fine grains, and soon the islands became more sparse, giving way to the thick upright stalks of leafy milfoil. As rocks became rare and stalks dense, Maggie began to swim between rocks and around plants, zigzagging in an overall downstream direction. But soon she stood on the edge of one rock looking for the next, and none was in sight. All she could see in the waning night light was a milfoil thicket with its floor piled deep in curled, fallen leaves.

Maggie looked at the streamscape for a long time. Jacob had left her ready to go find the riches of the stream; now she would have to wait for dawn. In disappointment, she roamed the surface of this last rock outpost and found a few scraggly blooms of short-stalked *achnanthes*. She ate the crispy diatoms and then hungrily swam upstream to another rock, where she scoured its surface and found a few more blooms. Maggie zigzagged back upstream, picking up a few bites here and there, until she was reasonably satisfied. Then she found a narrow crevice in the downstream face of a large, jagged rock and went to sleep.

The first rays of light woke Maggie, and, forgetting where she was, she banged her head on the roof of the narrow furrow. Somewhat dazed, she emerged from her sleeping chamber and climbed to the top of the rock.

Green stalks of milfoil surrounded her. From their heavy roots, round trunks towered upward toward the other world, exploding in a thick canopy of delicately dissected leaves. Fine, hair-like leaflets branched out from slender center stems, and long strands of green, blue green, and yellow algae draped among the branches.

The current quickly cleared Maggie's head, and she scurried down the rock and hurried downstream. Soon she was back at the border of the milfoil thicket, where a continuous blanket of golden and green leaf fragments covered the ground below the endless stalks.

Maggie spotted a covey of humpbacked sideswimmers foraging just inside the thicket. Not insects, the tall but narrow sideswimmers had legs on almost every segment, of which there were fifteen.

Maggie called, "Excuse me."

None in the pale, leggy group responded.

"Hello!" she called more loudly.

This time one of the sideswimmers looked up. He lowered the long strand of swollen *melosira* disks he had been eating. Two pairs of long antennae flopped carelessly over his face, and big black eyes peered out from over the lower pair. Instead of responding to Maggie, though, the sideswimmer nudged his closest companion. The companion looked up and likewise nudged his neighbor. Then each sideswimmer proceeded in turn to nudge his neighbor until the entire group was looking at Maggie. Finally, one replied casually, "Hello."

"Hello," Maggie repeated and then nodded quickly several times to greet each of the noncommittal, light green and white faces. "I was wondering if any of you might know just how far downstream it is to rocky terrain."

"Oh, just a stroll," a different one said, and then they all began to giggle. The broad bases of the first of their thirteen pairs of legs hid their mouths from view.

"It will take you the better part of daylight to get there," a sideswimmer with stout antennae offered after having enjoyed Maggie's predicament sufficiently.

"What is the terrain like?" Maggie asked her.

"Oh, it's nice—ample food and ready refuge," she replied. Then pointing to the mounds of leaf litter surrounding them she added, "Just like this." The sideswimmers all started tittering again and rolled around on their pillow of detritus.

Once the sideswimmers were through giggling, Maggie thanked them politely, pretending she was indifferent to the prospect of a day's walk through belly-deep detritus. She then swam from their sight, but once beyond their view, she set down and started to walk. The thicket really was too dense to swim through.

Maggie tromped past shoot after shoot of upright and bowed, thick-trunked and thin-trunked, tall and short, flush and stark milfoil. Her path meandered, as the haphazard arrangement of stalks made a straight course impossible. Yet the light of the other world gave the thicket a pleasant green hue, and the waters moved freely through the milfoil, the pliant stalks bending gently aside to allow passage. Small *microthamnion* and *stigeoclonium* bushes grew upon the thick stalks, and glassy needles of *synedra* and ribbons of filamentous algae rested among the wispy leaves. In its lightness, its fullness, and its softness, Maggie actually found the reach to be quite pleasant—only this muck she had to plow through, having to pull her legs above it at each step, made the walk tiring. A steady stream of leaf fragments floated in her wake.

At the swollen base of one lean stalk, Maggie stopped to rest. She arched her back and stretched her gills out into the current. Just then, a rain of leaf bits fell down on her. She brushed the flakes from her head and shook them from her back, yet no sooner had she finished doing so when the milfoil swayed slightly and another shower of debris fell on her. Taking the flurry to be a wave in the current, Maggie brushed the flakes off again. After the third such dusting, though, she looked up.

Amid the lower branches of the lean stalk, a silken sack, with a few strands of yellow-green *oedogonium* woven in, was moving about. It wasn't going anywhere but was extending and retracting itself vigorously in every direction. With a violent shaking of the sack, a small caddisfly emerged from the opening of this silken case shouting, "You stupid sack!

Stay there if you'd like—I'm sick of you anyway! What do I need you for?" And as if to convince his case of the finality of his resolve, he pushed it forcefully with his forelegs, turned away, and came marching down the stalk in a huff, straight toward Maggie.

Seeing her there, he demanded, "What are you looking at, eh?"

Maggie, embarrassed that she had been caught staring, replied, "Nothing."

"Well thanks a lot," the caddisfly pursed his palps. "I've always thought myself a rather dashing fellow."

"Nnnnnnnnno," stammered Maggie, "I didn't mean—"

"You didn't mean to see that scene?" the petite caddis asked. "Well, that's all right. I have nothing to hide. In fact, that's why that old rag can stay right where it is, and I'm going on my way naked. Yes, naked," he announced in defiance to the milfoil. "Look at her," he called to his sack; "she doesn't drag around some silly wrap."

"Yes, but I'm a bit more hard-skinned than you," Maggie pointed out.

"Well, that flimsy silken sack I wear is certainly not any protection," he said with disdain, looking over his back at it. "It's not like I have the skills to build a sturdy case of grain. I'm just a joke—I can hardly swim, and I have a silk sack that gets caught on every darn twig I pass. So why not walk naked? Now, if you would step aside for a moment—the lymph is rushing to my head, and I would like to get down."

Maggie hopped aside to allow this impudent caddisfly passage. His crass manner, though, made him more curious than offensive. Maggie actually thought the caddisflies to be some of the most elegant individuals of the stream. Elaborate designs drawn with contrasting browns, tans, yellows, and blacks decorated their heads and thoraxes; the shapeliest of legs were graced with long, curving claws; and shiny, round heads sported the most subtle of palps, antennae, and eyespots. In addition, a variety of modest to quite elaborate cases of silk, stick, leaf, and rock adorned their variably warty, variably expanded, soft-skinned posteriors.

The caddisfly, on the streambed again, spent a few minutes unabashedly primping, seemingly oblivious to Maggie. With his claws, he brushed detritus from the bristles on his head and then oriented each one into the position he preferred. He was particularly fussy about the bristles along the perimeter of a dark brown patch in the middle of his forehead. The rest of his head was light brown, except for the soft yellow streaks that encircled his small, black eyes and extended all the way back to a dark brown collar at the base of his head.

Once he had finished coiffing his head, the caddisfly attended his thorax; not the longest of legs stretched to clean and position the long bristles that arose from the hard, dark brown patches that covered most of his back. Next he rolled on his side, curled around his soft, fat, green abdomen, and cleaned the bristles there, right down to the hook at his very posterior.

Returning to his feet, the caddisfly rested his abdomen on a pile of leaf litter. "Have you ever thought of how very ridiculous we are put together?" he asked. "Look at me," he directed, hugging his thorax with his midlegs. "The legs that carry me to and fro are all up here, while behind them trails this—duffle bag." He slapped his pudgy abdomen. "You'd think these balloons would keep us humble," the caddisfly sighed, glancing down at his foreclaws, "but who is humble nowadays?" He commenced cleaning his claws and asked, "Who are you, anyway?"

"Maggie."

"And what's a Maggie?"

"A mayfly," Maggie replied, confused by the question. "And you are?" she asked politely.

"A joke. I told you that already. ..." He glanced up at her. "A hiccup. A wake up. But you can call me Trichop. Think how much better off we'd all be," he said, returning to his claws and pulling plant debris out from their grooves, "if we didn't have these clumsy abdomens to drag around behind us. Instead, we could be little beasts scurrying around on our six little legs." Apparently liking the idea, Trichop lifted himself onto the tips of his claws, lifted his chubby, green abdomen as best he could, and began to prance about the mounds of fallen leaves as if weightless. His abdomen swung wildly from side to side, and soon his effort exhausted him.

When he slowed down, Maggie reminded him, "The essentials for our future are in our abdomens. What would be the point of being little creatures of legs scurrying about if there were no eggs, no future?"

"And what do you think we are anyway?" Trichop demanded, his antennae raised and his palps distended. "We're little egg sacks scurrying about! Tell me, where are you scurrying?"

"I'm *walking* downstream," Maggie said emphatically and then looked in that direction. All she could see was more milfoil.

"Downstream." Trichop looked there too. "And what's downstream?" he asked, turning back. "Hmm, hmm," he prodded her, his shiny, bristly head thrust forward.

"Well," Maggie had to admit, "I'm not exactly sure."

"Nothing for certain, I'm sure, I'm sure," Trichop sang gleefully and swung his abdomen from side to side, hollowing out a swath in the leaf litter. "So why are you going there?"

"Well, where should I go?" Maggie said, becoming a bit annoyed by this inquest.

"Glad you asked!" Trichop said and stepped back to give full field to his forelegs. "As I figure it, nowhere. Yes, nowhere. Insects going upstream," he threw one foreleg upstream; "insects going downstream," he threw the other downstream; "upstalks," his head went up; "downstalks," his head went down; "and where are they all going?" he asked, throwing his head and forelegs in every direction. Yet it was obvious he had no intention of waiting for an answer. "As if downstream takes them someplace they haven't been before." He brought his face up against Maggie's. "And why are you walking downstream?"

"I'm looking for a good patch," Maggie's words rushed out, her feeling a bit put on the spot.

"And tell me," Trichop continued without pause, "what does a good patch look like?" He backed up against a milfoil stalk, rested his abdomen on its broad base, and with a foreclaw, began to stroke a particularly long bristle just beside his mouth. Glints of bright light reflected from his hard head.

Having been asked about her patch several times of late and having just had a long walk in the muck during which she had ample time to think of her destination, Maggie had just the place in mind. "In perfection, a good patch would have not just one sort of algae, but a tasty variety; the forage would be thick and free from sediment; and the patch would be located in a terrain of broad, flat rocks with steady, well-aired waters. And, if it were to be really perfect, the patch would be so rich and large that I would never have to leave it. Yes, that would be perfection, to have all those good things in one place." Her foreleg stretched downstream, ready to go find the place of which she spoke.

But the caddisfly wasn't finished. "Hope," he said softly; "hope for an illusion you see more clearly than the world before your face." His voice rapidly crescendoed. "Why are we made these jokes—these inconsequential bodies feeding, moving, risking all for a few glorious moments we might not even see?"

"But it is our purpose," Maggie broke in to defend her vision, "to forage toward our maturation."

"Purpose—urpose—rpose—pose—ose—se—e—" Trichop recited, throwing his head from side to side. "There. Got rid of that," he said in staccato. "A fiction. If there is purpose, then why is the stream of the nature it is?" he asked. "Why do currents change without warning, taking us to wherever they please, putting us far from where we would ever want to be?" The small caddisfly strolled among the milfoil as he talked to Maggie and whomever else might be listening. "You want a place of flat rocks and steady flow— how long will the stream let such exist? It doesn't promise us a forever, nor for that matter any future." He stopped in front of Maggie. "Of that you can be certain." And with this statement he laughed and again threw his chubby abdomen from side to side as he sang, "for certain, for certain.

"Yes," he continued, barely stopping to breathe, "certainty. When we see something happen over and over, we latch on to it. 'Ah! The rhythm of the stream,' we say. But the unpredictable? We back away from it." To dramatize his point, he backed away from Maggie, and apparently finding walking backward amusing, he continued to do so while he talked. "Faced with the unpredictable, we throw up our claws and say it is without reason.

"Yet it's reasonless events that bring mayflies underfoot," he declared upon coming full backward circle and bumping into Maggie. He looked over his back at her and said, barely audible, "Don't you see? The stream doesn't tell us when it's going to roll us into little balls, our heads touching our tails, and toss us into the drift." He turned around to face her. "Random events shape our lives, our fate—and you want to pretend we have a purpose?" The caddisfly shook his head and walked away. "Why can't we accept that it is a random, unpredictable world in which we live; that we are only little beasts with whom the stream plays frolic; that our direction is, in the larger order of randomness, arbitrary?" He was almost shouting.

"The stream tumbles and tosses, carries and displaces, but goodness, we have claws with which to grasp the ground, our legs on which to stand," Maggie held. She wasn't about to allow this small, doubting caddisfly dislodge her from her mooring.

Trichop was busy ascending a tall pile of leaves. Once upon the summit he said, "No doubt you're determined to direct where the stream takes you."

"I plan to resist currents that would take me where I don't want to go. We're all built to resist the current somewhat."

"Somewhat," he pushed her paltry effort down the mound with a flip of his foreclaw, "but our success is minimal, our efforts futile. We want to guide our destiny, so we weave a delusion that we have some control. But we don't, for we are little twits in a big stream that controls with abandon. We react, we respond, we try to salvage our egos, for none of us wants to be tossed about so inconsequentially."

Maggie looked up at the caddisfly who, having just abandoned his case, stood elevated in his brown and green nakedness and bit into the world with his piercing mandibles.

"We needn't be tossed about inconsequentially," Maggie resisted his overbearing current; "we have a great deal of opportunity to go where we want, to make choices about how we live."

"Choices?" Trichop queried as if he had heard a new word. "Choices!" he shouted. "I can go wherever I please!" he yelled and ran down the hummock in found liberation. "If I give up eating," he said in a coarse voice when he reached the bottom. "This milfoil doesn't grow everywhere, you know. It's not like I can go just anywhere to find these gold and green noodles I eat," he said, pointing to the tender filaments of *oedogonium* growing on the milfoil stalks. "How can you talk about choice when we are so confined by our habits, our needs, when we can be eaten at any unforeseen moment, when a feckless stream decides our fate?!"

"There are uncertainties, risks, necessities, but we need not be subjects of the vagaries of the current," Maggie insisted. From where had this contentious caddisfly come in the midst of her travels to a rich reach? She was getting hungry, but she felt compelled to convince Trichop they were not incapable of directing their paths. "It's easiest to go with the flow," Maggie said, "but if we don't stand up to the current, well, we'll all pile up downstream."

"So what difference does it make," Trichop asked, "tell me, what difference does it make whether you tell yourself you're choosing to stand and then are carried off by the current rather than simply allowing yourself to be carried off in the first place? We end up on the same piece of ground." He latched his foreclaw into a stalk and hung from it limply. "You arrive thinking you have chosen, while I arrive having let the stream choose for me—without illusion. Do we look any different?" Trichop looked toward Maggie and then released the stalk and marched up to her. He stopped with his face just a bristle's length away from hers. "Yes, we do," he said, surprised at his own observation. "You look tired."

"But there's no freedom in allowing the stream to control your destiny," Maggie argued, exasperated.

"Freedom!" He pulled back. "Freedom!" He pulled back some more. "My dear mayfly, of wondrous things you sing. Freedommmm!" Trichop called, and with that he sprang from the ground and into the water column and started to drift among the stalks, composing:

> *"To trichop a lot is such a drag,*
> *to be bound up in an old silken rag."*

He caught the stem of a fat milfoil with his posterior claw and dangled from the plant, gleefully throwing his body from side to side, defying caution. Maggie scurried to catch up to him.

"What are you doing?!" she demanded, looking up into the thick canopy of frilly leaves and attendant algae.

He grabbed the stalk with his forelegs and released his hind claw. His body stretched out in the current.

"I am enjoying liberation from my shackles. My cousins with their splendid cases—Helio, Molanna, and Leptocerc with their fine cases of grain; Limno, Phrygae, and Brachy with cases woven from leaves and twigs. Their entire sense of who and what they are is tied up in those wraps of theirs. But do you know, beneath their fine cases, they all have soft, bulgy bodies—and they all have only six legs on which to stand. Yet still, they insist on fettering themselves with those weighty cloaks they carry."

Trichop released his grip, rolled up in a ball, and began to float. Immediately he bumped into a stalk. He grabbed the stalk with one set of legs, flung himself around it, and then propelled himself to another plant. He began vaulting from one milfoil to the next, reciting:

"Molanna has a case of grain,
how wondrous it is.
Shows her face and hides her gain,
preparing for her kids."

Grabbing another stalk, he continued:

"Helico has a case of distinction,
coiled like no other's.
Hence his body's coiled too,
separating him from his brothers."

Trichop laughed and laughed, quite pleased with himself, and then went on:

"Lepto a more subtle home,
meticulous and neat.
Hence his fine finesse is shown,
his image is replete.

"Limne's got a modest shack,
though neatly pieced together.
Made of fragments, silk, and tack,
to withstand the weather.

"Calamo a 'vulgar' shack;
they say 'has he no pride?'
Simply a wooden twig hollowed out
in which his body hides.

"Of my cousins who wander not,
and of those who wander freely,
from these I differ quite a lot,
and so I love them dearly.

"I, I have a case of silk
that only serves to bind me.
If it were not for mother dear,
I'd leave it all behind me."

"So you do feel some responsibility for your sack, don't you?" Maggie asked at his last words.

"I? I, who would abandon that rag, leave it forever; drift downstream, no threads attached; tie not my security to a rock or a case; sing amongst my fellows of today and not tomorrow—for what should I feel responsible?"

"For what you make of yourself, for what you contribute to the stream."

"If I have no control over my future, how can I be responsible for it?" Trichop let go of the stalk and began to float away. Maggie jumped up, grabbed his hindleg, and pulled him to the ground.

"Look at you!" she said, pointing out the refractory Trichop to himself. "You're *choosing* to toss away your case."

"Yes, and now I can't decide whether to reclaim that sack or litter the landscape with it." The caddisfly looked up at his case caught between two leaf stems and shook his head. Then he returned to the stalk, grabbed onto it, and began to climb. His graceful legs were actually quite strong, for they carried his rotund abdomen nimbly. When he reached his silken sack, he began to tug at it.

"If you're so willing to accept where the stream takes you, why aren't you willing to accept your case?" Maggie asked. She couldn't understand why he wanted to abandon the one thing that did allow him some means to guide his circumstance.

"Why must I accept a weight I don't want to carry? My case tells me where I may go and how; it binds me by my fancies, reminds me of my needs." He pulled a long silk thread from his case and dangled it in the current.

"You're shedding your case as if it isn't part of you, but the behaviors to build it are engrained."

Trichop looked down at Maggie. "My point exactly," he said, quite pleased. "Ex-act-ly. I want to transcend these predetermined behaviors, these false securities. I want to experience the stream raw bodied." He released the thread he held and pulled out another.

"And to transcend your limitations will you toss away the threads by which you weave yourself intact?"

"They are the same threads with which we weave illusions that keep us from seeing that the stream moves without purpose, that we are all too small to be of consequence. ... I want freedom from the delusion that I can affect a world too confusing to understand." He pulled another thread.

"It seems to me any freedom you'll gain from unraveling your case will quickly come undone," Maggie called from the base of the stalk. She waited but received no response. The atypically quiet Trichop was busy dismantling his sack: he grabbed clawfuls of silk and released them into the current. Maggie tried shaking the milfoil to get his attention, but the base of the stalk was too heavy to be moved.

"How will you find the freedom you want if you don't accept your ability to affect its fabric?" Maggie asked. "Isn't it through maintaining our own integrity that we maintain that of the stream? And isn't it in the fine, pliant fabric of the stream's well-being that our own freedom truly rests?"

"Oh, what a tangled mess you weave," said Trichop, hanging upside down by his posterior claw and waving threads of silk in the current with his foreclaws. The bottom half of his case was completely torn away.

"Even the sponge, anchored to her boulder, having only what the stream brings her, chooses when to accept, when not to—"

"So is that freedom?!" Trichop grabbed the stalk with all his legs and began to descend. "Engaging in a futile process called choice?!" He stretched onto the streambed. "Choices to come out of a potpourri of fragments whose origin we can't even identify," he shouted, tossing leaf bits up into the water. "How can we pretend to make good choices, wise choices, when we reach blindly into such a sack of confusion?"

"Look at you!" Maggie pointed to his tattered silk remnant. "We are creatures who choose; even if we make our choices in the midst of a capricious current, we don't have the choice of no choice."

"And that is the cruelest joke," Trichop said and kicked a mound of detritus. He then walked to the milfoil at the mound's center and tried to shake the plant's massiveness.

Maggie watched Trichop as he pushed against stalks that offered gentle resistance to his vigorous protestations. In fast waters, if he didn't grasp the ground firmly with his claws, he would be washed away. The waters of the stream would carry him unknowingly, and he would be as effectorless as he aspired to be. Maggie thought of Teresa again, whose only choice was to encrust herself when waters became inhospitable. "For all of us," Maggie said to Trichop, "our success at holding our ground depends on the stream being benign."

"Just what I said!" Trichop grabbed his point back. "All these legs just make light of the fact that we have no firm ground to stand on."

"No. Not at all!" Maggie stamped her claws in objection. She could not yield him this. "The stream is not just a flood of fast waters. We all have some means to stand our ground in a current that can wash us away. It is when we forsake maintaining our integrity that we are abandoned to the stream's vicissitudes."

Trichop was again ascending the stalk that held his sack. He stopped abruptly and peered down at Maggie. "Where is your home mayfly? Several night lights upstream—in a pool still there?"

If my pool were still there as I left it, Maggie thought.

"You want a reason to stand on that is more stable than the rock you were washed from," Trichop concluded. He grimaced, his palps distended, and shook his head. He held the stalk by one claw.

"If we are not torn adrift, can't we direct our wanderings?" Maggie asked.

"You," Trichop said, "you are a drifter of hope, whereas I, I am a drifter of whim." And with that the caddisfly released his grasp, rolled up in a ball, and liberated himself into the drift.

"Stop!" Maggie shouted, running after him. "You can't! The fish!"

Trichop continued floating downstream, high up in the fringed canopy. He bumped into stalks and rolled off them; leaves bent gently aside.

Maggie stopped and watched as he floated away. She did not know if he would remain intact while going wherever the current might take him. Yet neither was she certain where directing her own path might lead her.

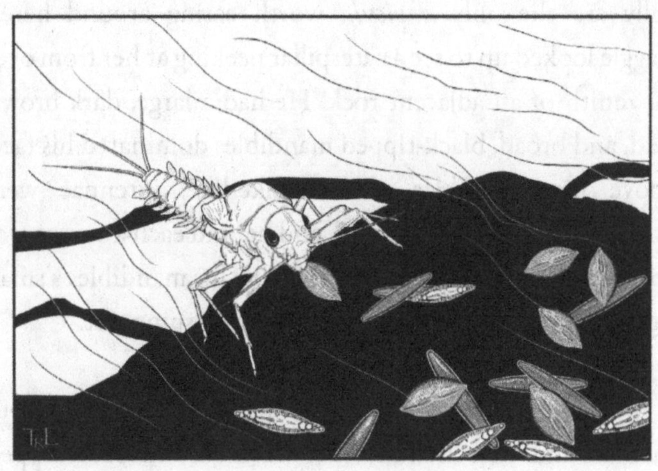

CHAPTER EIGHT

FELLOW FINE FOOD FORAGERS

After a full day's tromp through the milfoil thicket, Maggie found that as rocks had given way to milfoil, milfoil finally thinned to give way to rocks: nice rocks—smooth, rounded hills—not broad, flat plateaus but still a welcomed relief. Glassy, yellow diatoms donned the rocks, and Maggie foraged far into the night light. The steady flow of the milfoil thicket fanned out over the rounded reach.

In the light of early morning, Maggie climbed to the top of a high hill and looked downstream. Before her she saw a stretch of smooth, tan stones dotted with clusters of green and golden algae. Happily she made her way to the closest of these eateries and was snacking on some long, spindle-shaped diatoms when a sonorous voice remarked, "*Tripunctatas* really are the only *navicula* worth eating around here." Maggie looked up to see a caterpillar peeking at her from over the zenith of an adjacent rock. He had a large, dark brown head, and broad, black-tipped mandibles dominated his face. Above his mandibles, short, spike-like antennae were separated by his wide forehead, and behind each antenna was a ring of six small black eyespots. Below his mandibles a small spout protruded; it was his silk-producing spinneret.

"They are very good," Maggie agreed.

So invited, the caterpillar momentarily disappeared to walk around the circumference of the rock. He stopped across from Maggie, on the other side of a shallow gully. With an ochre-green, soft, tubular abdomen, he reminded Maggie somewhat of Rensaleer, but his abdomen was much broader than Rensaleer's, and a myriad of thread-like gills adorned the length of his sides. The first segment of his thorax was as dark as his head, making his large head look even larger.

"I really do prefer *tripunctatas* over most of the other *naviculas*," the caterpillar said, "don't you?" His gills spread out in the current like dancing worms.

Tripunctatas were one of Maggie's favorites. "Yes," she replied, "I do like them."

The caterpillar relaxed his cylindrical abdomen into an informal bend. "They have a subtle taste, but once you've learned to appreciate it, *tripunctatas* are the only diatoms that have it, don't you think?"

"Now that you mention it, I guess so," Maggie concurred.

"Oh, definitely," said the caterpillar, his head bobbing up and down, happy to corroborate his observation.

"I suppose that's why they're so hard to find," Maggie surmised; "they're so particularly good."

"You know, though," said the caterpillar in a voice lowered in confidentiality, "*tripunctatas* are also eaten by many grazers who have no real appreciation of them. Some rather indelicate fellows will down them just as if they were some ordinary *radiosas*. That kind of grazer doesn't even savor the taste, do you know what I mean? Doesn't that really get you?" He vented a snorting laugh and bobbed his head some more.

"When I think of how much time I spend looking—" Maggie considered, "yes, it certainly is frustrating to think of someone gobbling down *tripunctatas* so unappreciatively."

With another snorting laugh and bobbing of the head, the caterpillar commented, "Those who can eat anything eat everything indiscriminately, whereas those of us who savor our morsels are left searching the harder. But such is the stream," the smooth voice yielded, "so I just look longer for the finest."

"So do I," Maggie blurted out.

"Really! That's great!" The caterpillar's head bounced vigorously in enthusiasm. "Fine foods make the difference in one's flight, don't you think?" he asked.

"Oh, yes!" Maggie said excitedly at the mention of this event.

"I am very particular about my diet," the caterpillar confided. "I feel I must nourish upon the richest of foods now, for while still an immature, I shall stop feeding," he told an attentive Maggie. "I shall build a case of silk around me, and in my cocoon I shall be quiescent while my very essence changes. When I reawake, I shall emerge into the world of air as a great, winged moth. With wings much larger than my body, wings covered with lush, colorful plates bright and beautiful, I shall fly high. I shall shine like the light of the other world, and so enlightened, my wings will be magnificent!"

Maggie was enthralled by the caterpillar's magical incantation. Yet she wouldn't undergo any such glorious transformation; her body changed gradually, even now with her growing wings apparent under her skin. Her adult wings would be transparent and fragile, with none of the colorful adornments of which the caterpillar spoke.

"My wings will not be so grand," she told the caterpillar, "but still I yearn for rich foods. I've traveled a good distance, looking for a reach of lush fields. But so far, I've found only bits and pieces. The real problem, though," Maggie said, feeling that this caterpillar was willing to share the ins and outs of foraging with her, "is that I'm never sure if I'm giving up too hastily. Sometimes all there is to be had isn't readily found—one needs to go back through a patch and take a closer look. But then, one can spend a lot of time looking and come up with nothing more. I'm always in a bit of a quandary as to when I should move on and look for something better."

The caterpillar had listened attentively, his head nodding in understanding. When Maggie finished speaking, he replied with speedy ease, "It's simple. You want to evaluate your net profit against your estimate of alternative investments based on an integrated composite of previous nets with particular weight given to recent trends."

"What?"

"Straightforward," the caterpillar said, his body easing into a sag. His gills were made immobile where his body folded. "Each patch has some absolute value, you see, that is determined by the forage that is there. But of course you have to discount its value based on your costs, such as the distance you had to travel to get to the patch." He shifted his weight, relieving the compressed gills. "So the patch's value over such costs gives you your net yield. When you contrast this return to a composite of your returns on recent experiences," the caterpillar continued in a tone of self-evident clarity, "you can determine when it's time to look for a new patch."

"Is that how you decide where to eat?" asked an amazed Maggie. She hadn't quite followed all the estimating, discounting, and compositing, but this caterpillar seemed to understand how it all worked.

"Oh yes. Where and what."

"I don't think I could."

"Oh, it's really simple," the caterpillar said, his head and forebody bobbing. "Why don't we go find a patch, and I'll show you."

"If you don't mind," Maggie said politely, hoping he wouldn't.

"Hey, what's life about anyway? It's just great to meet another grazer who appreciates fine foods. Let's go this way— I just came through those boulders."

Although the caterpillar had an abundance of legs, his gait was slow. His body moved forward in a slow ripple: three pairs of short, clawed legs on his thorax navigated his path, while five pairs of short, fleshy legs on his abdomen sought to find footing through the exact same route as his forelegs.

Stopping frequently, the caterpillar would anchor himself to the ground with the fine hooks of his fleshly legs and then lift his forebody above the streambed to peer ahead. Each of his movements was deliberate; none was made needlessly. For Maggie, whose movements were somewhat frenetic, this caterpillar's well-placed steps were enviable.

"I like this—" remarked the caterpillar as they passed whorls of the finely beaded branches of an olive *batrachospermum* bush, "traveling along with a fellow fine food forager, looking for fine food together."

"So do I," agreed Maggie, liking the idea of being a fellow fine food forager. "Searching for one's forage alone, it's easy to think that one has little in common with others in the stream. Yet there's so much we have in common—the waters, the desire for good food, and," except for a recalcitrant caddisfly Maggie thought to herself, "the desire for a productive life."

"And then you and I share even more in common," the caterpillar pointed out, "as we seek the same kind of food. Look, over there," he said, peering from above. "A bloom of *cymbella*, isn't it?"

"Sure is," Maggie said and started to bolt. But she immediately slowed and waited politely for her companion.

Golden crescents of *cymbella*, swaying in the current on tall, gelatinous stalks, marked a large and fertile field of algae.

"I start by making a quick assessment of the value of the patch," the caterpillar said at the edge of the field. "I transect the patch, and along the swath I cut, I inventory the food items. So let's proceed." The caterpillar brought his last pair of legs up to his first pair, causing the rest of his body to rise as a loop high above the ground. As he walked forward assessing the forage, his body returned to the substrate, segment by segment. Maggie followed him closely and listened attentively so that she could learn how to conduct a patch evaluation.

"Six *cymbellas*, two *naviculas*, three *closteriums*..." he called. Once fully elongated, the caterpillar scurried his hindlegs back up to his fore, forming another loop to be unbowed. "Seven *achnanthes*, one *gloeocapsa*, two more *naviculas*..." he continued. In that manner they crossed the patch, the caterpillar looping and elongating until they reached the far edge ten of his long body lengths later. There the caterpillar instructed Maggie: "Now each type of forage is ranked according to its quality. Stalked and loosely attached diatoms get four points whereas diatoms that are appressed to the substrate, like *cocconeis*, get only two points. Bluegreen and green algae not in filaments get three points, unless, of course, they are too large—but that goes without saying for everything. Young or tender filaments, like *spirogyra* or *microthamnion*, get two points, whereas any long or tough filaments get one point. So, we have five *gomphonemas* times four, three *gloeocapsas* times three..." He continued to multiply and sum until he concluded, "which gives us, in total, 664 food points for this transect.

"Now, let's see." The caterpillar lifted his forebody and peered about. "I would estimate the width of this patch to be equivalent to eighteen transects, so 18 times 664 gives us 11,952 food points as the total food item value of the patch," he deftly calculated. "Very good. Now, I've walked about sixty-five body lengths, can you believe it, from the last patch

I visited, so we multiply 65 times 10, the food unit conversion factor, which gives us 650. Because there are two of us, we'll double our T—that's my notation for travel costs—which gives us 1,300. We multiply this times R—"

Maggie, already lost but trying to follow, asked, "R?"

"A habitat-dependent constant," the caterpillar mumbled, in the midst of his calculations, "and we get 2,600. So we can yield about 12,000 food units for a cost of 2,600 units; our ratio of return is 4.6. Very good." His nodded vigorously. "The average for my last three experiences, 2.5, 2.3, and 2.7 is 2.5. Now, what we want to do," the caterpillar leaned toward Maggie to instruct her carefully, "is forage this patch until its value is reduced to being no better than average. At that point, an investment of our time elsewhere could yield a better return. So this patch, at 4.6, yields a return 2.1 times, our travel costs that is, above the average return of 2.5. Two point one times our travel costs is 5,460 food units, which means, simply put, that if we eat all the four-point diatoms, all the nonfilamentous greens and bluegreens, and some two-pointers—I suggest some *microthamnion*—which together total approximately 5,400 units, we'll maximize our gains from this patch."

"I'll never be able to remember all that!" Maggie said, dismayed.

"Don't worry about it—just eat." The caterpillar held open his short forelegs to welcome her to their feast.

And so they ate. And whereas the caterpillar was a slow and deliberate walker, he was a quick and deliberate forager. Pivoting on his hindlegs, he made a circle with his body and systematically foraged within it. His broad, flat head moved in a sweeping radius from the center of this circle to its circumference and then back from the circumference to the center along another line. With his large mandibles, he chewed his food quickly, and he gleaned from the rocks only those items that he had named. Maggie, on the other hand, bit into an oversized *cosmarium* if it were beside a *closterium* and ate a plump *cocconeis* if it were on her way to some ready-for-picking *achnanthes*.

When they had eaten all the choice greens, bluegreens, and diatoms, the caterpillar snorted, "Am I full!"

"So am I," Maggie laughed. "This is a great patch."

"Well, it was," the caterpillar said, "but now it's actually rather marginal. Recalculating our composite of returns, 2.3 and 2.7 from my last two patches, plus 4.6 for this patch, we obtain our new average ratio of return, 3.2, which is 0.7 points above the current value of this patch."

"I really don't understand these calculations," Maggie said. "May I tag along a while longer?" she asked hesitantly.

"Sure." The caterpillar bobbed his head and vented his snorting laugh. "Hey, if we're partners—my name is Pyralis."

"I'm Maggie."

"Why don't we look for another patch?" Pyralis suggested. "We can rest once we get there."

Following the path of a shallow trench, they cut across a wide, gray-brown rock. "Good meal, nice current, fine company," Pyralis commented; "what could be more pleasant?"

This walk in well-aired waters was pleasant to Maggie too. "I wonder why it has always seemed easier to me to forage alone," she asked.

"I guess we tend to do so," said Pyralis as he viewed the terrain ahead from above, "because at any one point it's easier to meet our own needs. And we must, after all," he continued, returning to the substrate, "ensure our own fulfillment."

"A few night lights ago I was in the company of a clan of stoneflies," Maggie told him. "To ensure their fulfillment, they all foraged together."

"And how did that work?" Pyralis asked, pausing mid-ripple.

"Well, I actually didn't stay very long. I didn't feel quite comfortable there, in the leaf pack."

"Well, some of us just need the airiness of open waters," Pyralis pointed out as he resumed his undulation. "You can't take a soul who needs a flowing current over her gills and put her in such a still."

"Yes, it just didn't feel right," Maggie said, warmed at being so readily understood. "And I quickly became hungry for some fresh greens. But it wasn't only that," Maggie remembered. "In the pack there was no room to explore the stream's workings for oneself; instead, each was told one's function as a cog in the greater design of the stream." Maggie slowed her steps to match Pyralis's pace. "Do you think we can all share some aspiration without all necessarily thinking the same way?"

"Well, we'll never all think the same way, will we?" Pyralis considered. "And I certainly wouldn't want to share any aspiration that denied me pursuing my own. Would you risk your enlightenment to be a cog?" he asked incredulously.

"Oh no!" Maggie hastened in response.

"Well, our foraging together should yield fruitful advantages," he concluded promisingly. Then peering ahead from an elevated vantage at a ridge of bare, pitted, pinkish rock, he commented, "Hmm. By my estimation, we should have reached another patch by now." Returning to Maggie's height, he shrugged. "Perhaps we're off in direction; we've come the right distance." He looked to the left and then to the right of where they stood and then shook his head. "One must be around here somewhere, but I need to rest awhile. Do you mind?"

"Of course not," replied Maggie.

"You walk so much faster than I can," Pyralis said as he stretched his abdomen out to its full length. "I'm sure you're used to getting where you're going in no time." His head began nodding as he looked at Maggie. "Hey, if you're not tired, maybe you could scout ahead while I rest for a few minutes."

"That's a good idea," Maggie agreed. She wasn't tired at all. "I'll come back to get you as soon as I find something."

"That would be really great," Pyralis said enthusiastically, his head bobbing full swing. "Yes, that would be very good. I'll be right there—in that crevice." He pointed to a ledge just above their heads.

So Maggie took off alone at her own gait. Slightly downstream of Pyralis, she reached a rise of black-flecked, pinkish stone. She followed the ridge to the right, searching in a wide swath until she reached its margin. Not finding anything substantial, she climbed over a low point in the ridge. On the other side, she started another transect back in the opposite direction. In this sweep, just downstream of the rise but well beyond where she had started, she found a patch about the same size as their last. She returned immediately for her foraging companion. She was tired now, though, for she had covered a fair distance since leaving Pyralis.

Pyralis was sleeping but awoke upon her approach.

"Did you find something?" he asked.

"Yes. There's a good size patch just about twenty of your body lengths downstream of here."

"Anything good?"

"I really didn't look it over," said Maggie, a bit embarrassed. She had in mind only to find it.

"Well, that's okay. We'll see what's there to eat when we get there. My, my," Pyralis yawned, stretching, "I really needed that. Just a little nap gives me a chance to assimilate all the fine food I've taken in for my grand transition. My, my," he stretched again. Then, crawling down from the crevice, he asked, "Are you ready to go?"

"Sure," said Maggie, "although I think I'll be ready to assimilate soon."

With Maggie knowing the route to the next patch, Pyralis forwent his predilection for peering ahead. Instead he was a constant wave of motion, hindlegs never quite catching up. Maggie scurried alongside him.

"There's the patch." Maggie pointed to it from the top of the ridge. A glimmering green and yellow field lay in plain view atop smooth, gray rock. Several thick, dark green *ulothrix* plants waved in the current.

At the edge of the patch Pyralis proceeded as before. "Three *naviculas*, two *nitzschias*, two strands of *spirogyra*," and so on, until they finished the transect. "The grand sum for the transect is 814, times, let's see—Maggie, would you scurry across the patch and determine its width?" While Maggie did so, Pyralis continued, "Thirty-three body lengths to our rest stop and 17 more to here equals 50 body lengths since the last patch, times 10 is 500, times the two of us is 1,000, times R is 2,000. Maggie, do you have the width?"

"Fourteen transects," called Maggie.

"So, 814 times 14 is 11,396; 11,400 to 2,000 is 5.7—that's good—and 5.7 is 2.5 above our composite. Very good. Two point five times 2,000 is 5,000, which means we should eat ..." there were a few moments of silence while he completed his computations, "the choice diatoms, bluegreens, and greens."

Maggie started foraging where she stood, on a soft, small ball of chartreuse *chroococcus*. She looked forward to a nap. This formula foraging was hard work, although they certainly were eating only the finest. Maggie thought she could feel her body purifying already. She bit into another *chroococcus*.

The bluegreen algae had such thin, soft walls, yet inside such a hearty flavor. The greens were tasty too, but their fibrous walls took much more chewing. The silica sheaths of diatoms made these algae somewhat brittle, but one could snap a diatom's wall or squeeze it to get to the sweet, golden center.

Once Maggie and Pyralis had eaten all the choice algae, Pyralis recalculated their composite of returns to be 4.2. "My, we're really experiencing a positive trend," he told Maggie and was ready to move on. But Maggie wanted to rest first, so they both nestled beside a log, just downstream of the patch.

Pyralis's stretching woke Maggie.

"Well hello there," he said. "Hope I didn't wake you." He shook his gills.

Maggie didn't answer; she was groggy from her deep sleep.

"I thought it might be prudent to find our next patch," Pyralis said.

Maggie, remembering the twists of *spirogyra* left behind, suggested they first return to their last patch for a snack.

"Oh, no," Pyralis said. "We shouldn't forsake our foraging strategy midstream and fall to seemingly easier paths. We must continue to seek only the finest of foods."

"You are very true to your pursuit," observed Maggie as they climbed over the log to continue downstream.

"My path must be sure if I am to meet my fulfillment. Otherwise, I might lose myself in meandering."

"I've done a great deal of that," admitted Maggie. She looked at the peaks before them, diverging formations jutting up against the horizon. "I suppose I've never seen a sure path. There are so many possibilities that sometimes I'm uncertain as to what my fulfillment even looks like."

"I've always been able to see the day when my wings will materialize," Pyralis said confidently. "That day my pursuit of fine foods will be manifested, and all I have foraged for will be apparent. My wonderful wings, their colors dancing in the light, will take me to mingle with the lofty heights of denselessness. Soaring through light and air, I shall know beauty; I shall be illuminated." He lifted his forebody up into the current and stretched his gills out in an arc. "So my path here is straightforward: garner as much good nourishment as possible and stay out of trouble."

"But what do you do when you find yourself in a poor reach?" Maggie asked.

"I cover my travel costs and move through it as quickly as possible."

She laughed.

"What's so amusing?" Pyralis asked, returning his forelegs to the ground.

"Myself. When I'm in a really bad reach, I drift."

"You purposely release the substrate and let yourself go in the current?!"

"Yes."

"I've never been in the drift," he quickly established. "To risk dislodgement, to have to grasp ground anew," Pyralis reflected, "one can never know where, *if*, one may set one's claws firmly down again. To land anywhere, in any reach, to be carried by rushing water—one might never regain control. One could be lost forever." He shook his head vigorously in disinclination. "No, I wouldn't want to risk losing my footing."

"Don't you have to take chances sometimes," Maggie asked, "to find the richest of foods to grow your fine wings?"

"Oh no," he corrected her misconception. "I have to travel the stream carefully if I want to reach adulthood safely."

"But what do you do if you need to escape a reach filling with sediment—or a predator who is about to nab you?" she asked.

Pyralis vented one of his snorting laughs. "Simple. In the former case, one should evaluate the situation before it gets out of control, and in the latter case, predators are foremost to be evaded. If one has not managed to do so, there is trickery, and if that fails, I guess any escape strategy is acceptable. The point is to minimize the unpredictable."

Maggie shook her head. "The waters of the stream have never seemed predictable enough to me to guess what might be ahead."

"That's because you haven't been evaluating your net gain trend," Pyralis pointed out. "What is downstream isn't certain, but one can make good predictions based on probabilities implied by current trends. When you walk and don't drift, you can apply reliable estimates to all of your parameters. What is ahead of you won't be very different from what is behind you if you travel by claw."

Pyralis stopped abruptly and his skirt of gills rushed forward. "Maggie, you'll have to give me a few minutes. I need to rest."

Maggie stopped and undulated her gills. She was becoming tired too, perhaps because they were walking so slowly again. She pulled at an old, abandoned midge's net that still clung to the ground. The net brought to mind Trichop, who also saw the stream quite clearly. "I guess I'm too dense to evaluate a trend until I'm in the midst of where it has led me," she said. "I always seem to fear that some essential piece may be hidden, so I dawdle in uncertainty, afraid of being mistaken."

"It's vital to make the attributes of your situation explicit if you want to make reliable estimates by which to avoid adversities."

"Perhaps what I want interferes with my vision of what is. ..." The midge's net became unfastened and floated away. The caddisfly's stream was quite different from Pyralis's.

"I'm sorry I can't keep up with your pace," Pyralis called Maggie back to the immediate. "You must be ready to move on."

"No," said Maggie, "we can rest."

Pyralis relaxed into a comfortable sag. "Waiting around for a slowpoke like me must seem a waste of time, though."

"Oh, no," Maggie assured him. "We decided to find fine forage together."

"Yes, we did," Pyralis recalled cheerfully. "Hey, maybe you want to scout ahead again." He nodded at the idea. "The next patch can't be more than twenty-five body lengths from here; if you find it, we shall be feasting soon." He bobbed his head, and his gills bounced along.

"That seems reasonable," Maggie agreed, so she left him resting and took off downstream.

While Maggie walked, she thought about Pyralis. None of his explicit attributes spoke of the fine foods he ingested; he was a robust but rather inelegant looking streamling. That he would become a wondrous winged being in the other world was unrevealed. In the stream, how did qualities that allowed one to be airborne appear?

Maggie had to negotiate some difficult terrain: short, steep peaks one after another. Approaching the distance Pyralis had estimated, she again employed a strategy of making a sweeping arc across the inner stream's width. Her transect took a great deal of time, for the terrain was a rocky rubble, and the width of the inner stream was even greater than the distance she had already come. The fractured stone she traversed was largely barren, and finding only *cocconeis* plastered to the substrate and *achnanthes* growing in deep crevices, she made another arc a bit farther downstream. There she found only more of the same. Frustrated by her search, Maggie decided to return for Pyralis before going on. She embarked on a direct route back to where she had left him.

Just downstream of where Pyralis rested, Maggie squeezed through a narrow gap and unexpectedly found herself on the edge of a broad, flat plain that was covered with diatoms: club-shaped *gomphonemas*, long, lanceolate *naviculas*, fat, oval *achnanthes*, and a few curled *gyrosigmas*. Relieved, Maggie stopped and ate a *gyrosigma* but then reminded herself that she should fetch Pyralis.

When she arrived she found Pyralis untangling a knot in his gills.

"My!" he called out when he saw her. "You've been gone quite a spell—I'd begun to worry."

"I've been walking my claws off," Maggie complained. "I went to where you estimated the patch would be and searched over the stream breadth twice without finding anything. I decided to come back for you before going any farther."

"You mean you didn't find a patch?" Pyralis asked with concern.

"Not there. But on my way back I took a different route and ran into one not sixteen body lengths from here."

"Whew!" Pyralis said, relieved. "I'm famished!"

His gait on their short walk was brisk, his energy restored.

"That this patch is closer than I estimated may be a good sign," Pyralis suggested in encouragement to a quiet Maggie. "It may represent an improving trend in resource quality. This depends on what's there, of course."

When the patch came into view, they were both dismayed to see a couple of immature riffle beetles grazing in the middle of the field. Pyralis hastened to reach them.

"Hi there," he greeted the beetles casually. "How's the current been?"

The beetles stopped foraging and lifted faces embossed with tufts of setae.

"Pretty good," the more setaceous of the two responded.

"Been here long?"

"No, just arrived."

"How are the pickings?"

"Good. Lots of *achnanthes*, some *gomphonemas*." The beetle pointed to some of the latter.

"Looks decent." Pyralis nodded, affably unimpressed. "We've been having a great day," he told them and pointed to Maggie, "spots rich with *gomphonema*, *cymbella*—so much forage, we ate only a fraction of it."

"Really? Where's this?"

"Just upstream of here—I haven't walked very far from our last patch at all. It was full of ripe diatoms, plump *gloeocapsa* balls, and fluffy strands of *spirogyra*." Lifting his forebody to look around, Pyralis said, "This place is nice, but," he shook his head in discouragement, "it just doesn't compare. And it's not just the last patch," he said to the beetles as he returned to the ground; "we've been hitting them all day long, just upstream of here. So good, my friend and I decided we'd just keep making our way downstream." He again peered around shaking his head. "You should check out our last patch. I guess we'll continue on our way."

Maggie raised her palps, ready to object, but before she did the more setaceous beetle said, "Hmm, perhaps we should head upstream and take a look at this place. How do we get there?"

"Oh, simple," Pyralis said congenially. "On the other side of that slate gray rock is a gully. Take the gully till you run into the first perpendicular overhang. Follow the overhang to the left. A path along the cliff's base will lead you up onto a plateau. The patch is there, on the next rock."

"Well, thanks for the directions. We're much obliged."

"Have a good day," Pyralis said and started to walk downstream. He motioned to Maggie to join him. The beetles conferred for a moment and then headed in the opposite direction.

"It took me forever to find this patch!" Maggie objected when she reached Pyralis. "I'm hungry and tired. I'm not about to walk away."

"Oh, we're not," he reassured her. "We're just doing our estimate." He began, "Five *anacystis*, five *cocconeis*, three *naviculas*—Maggie, what's the width of this area? Twenty-five plus 16 is 41 body lengths ..." Pyralis mumbled to himself. He soon concluded, "Our ratio of return is 7.0, or 2.8 above the composite. We should eat the four-pointers, the three-pointers, and half the two-pointers—I suggest the young *stigeoclonium* sprouts and *microthamnion* bushes." Pyralis grimaced. "We probably wouldn't have to eat filaments at all if we'd been here first."

"It wasn't quite true," said Maggie.

"What's that?" asked Pyralis, already eating.

"What you told those beetles about our last patch."

"I didn't say anything untrue," Pyralis considered, munching on a thin, crispy stick of *nitzschia*. "Anyway," said Pyralis, "those beetles won't really miss the *gomphonema* and *cymbella*—it's all the same to them."

Pyralis returned to grazing. Maggie, hungry and not wanting to miss out on the diatoms, followed suit. Yet her thoughts kept returning to the riffle beetles, who didn't look so very different from Pyralis, arriving at a patch that was less than what they expected.

When Maggie and Pyralis finished the algae that Pyralis had selected, he was ready to leave, but Maggie felt an emptiness in her stomach.

"Well go ahead and eat some *cocconeis*," Pyralis conceded, "but they really are marginal in quality."

Maggie pulled a few of the oval diatoms from the branches of a *stigeoclonium* bush, but Pyralis's comment made her self-conscious. "I'm ready to go," she soon said; "these *cocconeis* don't taste very good."

"As I said," Pyralis commented, "you can't yield richness from poorness." Standing at the downstream border of the patch, Pyralis peered ahead at the stretch of rock rubble. "You shouldn't worry about the beetles' diet, you know; they'll never be able to become the graceful flyers that we will."

"Is it only our food that nourishes our flight?" Maggie asked after they had walked in silence for a while.

"What else is there?"

"Well, the way we go about garnering that food."

"It is the greater heights we are to attain that we must keep in sight; we shouldn't misfocus our attention on this place of the mundane and risk polluting our pure natures. If one has the constitution to soar in the world of air, one must concentrate on garnering the stream's finest. Fine food will yield strong wings with which we fly so high that the stream will not even be in sight."

"But if we want to attain great heights in the other world, mustn't every movement here be a flexing of the muscles that will take us into denselessness?" asked Maggie.

"When we are gliding through the lofty heights, our movements at this or that patch will be inconsequential. All of this will be gone." Pyralis brought his short forelegs out before him as if offering the stream to Maggie. His gills waved in the waters around him.

Maggie looked at the stream before her. Small islands of algae dotted a reach of heavily foraged, rugged hills.

"What of your children?" she asked. "They must spend their youth here, in the stream."

"Of course, and the fine food I've eaten will produce fine offspring."

"But between egg and emergence there is a long path. We can garner fine forage for our eggs, but what good will this richness be if our young do not find a stream of fine quality?"

"We cannot determine what the nature of the stream will be for our children. We each have to garner what we need from the stream and impart to our children the constitution to do likewise." Pyralis began to slow. "I'm sure your children will find the fine forage they need for a grand flight." He came to a standstill under the long, tapering branches of a mature *stigeoclonium* tree. "I'm sorry, but I guess all our chatting has taxed my energy budget. Even now I must take great care to conserve energy for my transition. We aren't very far from the next patch," he sighed and nodded his head downstream, "but I need to rest. If you want to go off on your own—you must have the swing of things by now." He looked away from Maggie. "Just leave me some decent forage."

"Oh, no," Maggie reassured him that she wouldn't be so rude as to abandon him after his efforts to teach her the rules of foraging optimally. But what he had said made her realize that she didn't have the "swing of things" at all. She had looked for patches and eaten while Pyralis had made all the computations; she hadn't applied herself to learning his calculating procedures. Deciding to effort to do so, Maggie said, "I'll go look ahead for us. I'll be right back."

"That would be really great." Pyralis's head bobbed in earnestness.

Maggie headed downstream with Pyralis's estimate of the distance to the next patch and began to keep count of the distance she walked. At first counting was fun, but soon it became monotonous. Whereas Pyralis could talk and keep count at the same time, if Maggie let her mind wander, she lost her count. This fine food foraging was quite demanding.

So occupied was Maggie by counting that she didn't even notice that she had entered her own terrain: a plateau of broad, flat-topped rocks washed by deep, steady waters. Here she soon found a welcoming golden patch. "I've walked thirty-five body lengths," she fixed the distance in her mind. "Now I'll measure a direct route back to Pyralis." With the same monotony, but the surety of knowing where her next meal lay, Maggie returned to fetch Pyralis. When she reached him, she proudly announced, "The patch is fifteen of your body lengths from here."

"Good. Not a long walk at all," Pyralis commented and then stretched out from the spot where he rested.

Maggie concentrated on Pyralis's calculations at the patch. At the end of their transect he summarized their inventory. "What is the width of the patch, Maggie?" Maggie crossed the patch counting. While she did so, Pyralis continued to compute: "30 times 10, times 2, times R is 1,200. And the width?" he asked when Maggie returned.

"Eighteen," she told him.

"Eighteen times 586 is ... 10,560. Therefore, our net return is 8.8, which is 3 above our current composite. Three times our T is 3,600. We should eat the choice diatoms and the three-pointers; we can even go light on the greens."

Maggie requested that he go over the computations again, so that she could learn them.

You *do* know how to get the total food points for the transect?" he asked.

"Yes."

"You *do* know how to estimate the food value of the patch: the transect value times the number of transects in the patch. Now compute the travel costs—you're just going to have to memorize the constants," he said, sounding a bit impatient.

"Okay."

"Well, we walked thirty body lengths from our last patch to reach this patch, so 30 times 10 is 300, times the two of us gives us a T of 600, times R is 1,200. The patch value, 10,560, is divided by 1,200 to give us our net return, or 8.8. Comparing our present net to our current composite net of 5.8, we are directed to consume three times our travel costs, or 3,600 food units. If we eat all the four-point diatoms and all the bluegreens, we will have consumed 3,708 food units, which is more than sufficient." Pyralis finished and turned to eating.

Maggie wanted to replicate these calculations. "Okay," she said to herself, looking across the field. "The estimated patch value is 10,560. Now we walked fifteen body lengths from where Pyralis rested, which means we must have walked fifteen body lengths before he rested. So we have 30 times 10, times the 2—but—that's wrong." She looked up and said to Pyralis, "I walked our last fifteen body lengths twice."

"Oh, yeah, I guess so. It doesn't matter; it won't really change our net return."

Maggie recommenced computing: "Thirty times 10 times 2, plus 15 times 10 times 1 is 450." Suddenly it dawned on Maggie. "Pyralis, I never told you the distance I traveled to find this patch."

"Why not?"

"Well, uh, you didn't ask."

"Well, how far was it?"

"Thirty-five body lengths."

"Well, that brings the travel costs up by another 350 food unit equivalents," Pyralis grimaced, not being particularly pleased about this.

"What about R?" asked Maggie.

"Oh, it's minimal."

"What is R though?"

"A constant," Pyralis mumbled, his mouth full of food.

"A constant for what?"

"For risk."

"Risk? How do you compute risk?"

"It's twice the value of T."

Maggie calculated: "Fifteen plus 15 plus 15 plus 35 equaled 80, times 10 was 800, times 2. ..." R wasn't minimal at all! Well, not for her. She also computed it for Pyralis.

"R may be small for you," she told him, "but it isn't for me. It makes our net return on this patch 4.8, which is below our current composite!"

"Well, I guess you should just recoup your travel costs here if that's the case. Your R doesn't change the value of the patch for me."

Maggie began to graze but was very troubled. She felt as if she had just been dislodged in deep waters. In all those patches they had visited, their calculations had been off. For her. She should have been eating more. No wonder she was feeling tired and hungry: she hadn't been eating enough. With all their foraging calculations, she hadn't been eating enough! She bit into a bouquet of *cymbella*.

And without calculations? Not only would she have eaten enough, but she would have eaten about the same things Pyralis had told her to eat. She wouldn't have had a forecast of what lay ahead and when it might arrive, but there would have been no less risk involved.

That unitless cost, risk—with movement in unchartered territory there is risk, and risk makes a patch less valuable. Whereas Pyralis discounted risk as minimal, it was risk to which he was most adverse. And Maggie? If anything, she underestimated it, fearing more missing the patch she sought.

Pyralis's equations worked well for him, though; he ate only the finest forage in the patch. Now Maggie realized that he faired so well because she had done most of the looking. Yet beyond fine food, Pyralis understood how important her flight was to her, how she looked toward the day of flying through denselessness. He wouldn't have neglected that aspiration; she must be missing something.

"Your equation, it hasn't been working quite right," said Maggie.

"It works perfectly well—you just didn't understand it," Pyralis said and returned to his foraging.

"Well, why didn't you correct me?"

"It was your concern to determine how the balance worked for you." He didn't look up.

"I thought you were teaching me how to forage wisely; I thought your computations were for the both of us," Maggie said, wanting to salvage her vision of their joint pursuit.

"I can't risk my fulfillment on a mayfly who has no conception of risk or travel time, who can wander endlessly." He looked up with disbelief at Maggie's naiveté. "I am to be a great winged creature. I must watch out for myself, of course."

Maggie grasped at the passing water. "You said a partnership would be advantageous to us. I thought we were to share in the efforts as well as the fruits."

With startling clarity Pyralis recalled his words, "Oh no. I said our foraging together should yield fruitful advantages. But if you're going to increase our costs and thereby force us to eat poorer items, then foraging together might not be worth my while."

"But I thought you meant—" Maggie tried to anchor herself.

"Don't infuse my words with your meanings," he chided her.

"You didn't take your own words to heart."

"How haven't I done so?" he asked, his face impenetrable.

"Words devoid of sincerity are dangerous things!" Maggie cried, angry and hurt.

"How can *you* judge my sincerity?" Pyralis asked. He moved over to a nice spread of glimmering *naviculas*; his gills fanned out around him.

"But you deceived me!"

"No," he shook his head. "You deceived yourself."

"In the other world, it won't be my vision of your splendor that will determine the heights to which you will fly. You will yield the sum of your equation."

Pyralis hugged himself in comfortable satisfaction. "Yes. And in the end the purest of foods will fulfill me with the loftiest of wings." He reached for a couple of *gomphonemas*, plucked them from the ground, and nibbled on their stalks.

"From larva to pupa to adult you are malleable in form but not in essence. Like sincerity—it's not mutable just because it's not concrete." She walked around a cluster of dark *rivularia* blades that separated them. "Perhaps in the stream, where all seems embodied, it is only the material that is readily assessed. But in the other world, where things with no body permeate all space effortlessly, will the material become transparent? Will you unfold lofty wings if the pathway to them is not in kind?"

"My path has been most elevated."

"You ensure the strength of your wings by taking advantage of others!"

Pyralis focused his eyespots on her. "You feed on the pabulum and take what you need like any of us. Do you think that reality is any different because you tell yourself that you are doing something else, something more, because you are a good Maggie?" Pyralis snorted, shaking his head. "You gave to me so that you could take from me. We all try to profit." He spotted a few curved *nitzschias* and moved toward them.

"If we each see the stream as for only ourselves, then one day we shall see ourselves scrambling for a sustenance that is rapidly dwindling. Shouldn't we protect what has sustained our own journey? Shouldn't we replenish those qualities that have given the stream its richness?"

"What a specious painting," Pyralis said, finishing the last of the thin, crispy *nitzschia*. "I can see your benevolent world." He lifted his forebody to mimic the scene. "'No, no, dear, you first—I've had my share—Please, I *do* insist!—I've really had enough.' Well, I've really had enough." He returned to the substrate. "How can you speak to me of deception? Do you think because you think lovely thoughts all will be lovely?" His head shook in disbelief. "How can you, a mayfly, who can be eaten by any predator, travel through the world as if you don't need to garner sustenance to live, as if you don't need to find the right rocks to walk on and safe crevices in which to hide? You rewrite the way of the world to make it palatable to you."

"And what of you?" Maggie defended. "Are you so different a creature? You too need freedom of movement to feed—"

"Precisely, and so I estimate my parameters for a safe passage."

"What is the balance to an equation that allows one to prosper from a partnership he won't help maintain?"

Pyralis responded with tried patience. "Maggie, we each have our own sense of the ideal: it is where we maximize our own fulfillment. Ultimately, one is promoting one's own equation whether one claims to do so in the name of goodness or not. Why should I compromise myself for your sense of right?"

"You compromised *me* by sending me out as scout!"

Pyralis swallowed a mouthful of *achnanthes*. "You were free to decide whether to return," he said as if Maggie were stupid not to have realized this. "I recall you being quite anxious to reap the rewards of my equation." Then, as if the realization dawned on him, he said with annoyance, "Don't hand me responsibility for your decisions." He drew his forebody up into the current. "I'm responsible to my own concerns, thank you." He stretched over the gray rock to another clump of the short but plump *achnanthes*.

"Are our skins so thick?" she asked Pyralis, turning toward him. "Will we emerge into the splendor of another world where the stream doesn't matter? To see ourselves above and beyond other streamlings makes them appear minute and inconsequential. If we are so seduced, our heart becomes corrupted by the vision of our own grandeur."

Pyralis snorted, his head bobbing while he finished chewing the last morsel of fine forage. "Your reality lies along some obtuse transect that goes somewhere you do not even know. It is a precarious path to crawl upon, for you repeatedly slide off. And since you can never see it, you're never even sure if you're on it." He snorted again. "My reality is much more straightforward: the stream is horizontal, and the other world is up." Looking through Maggie toward downstream, Pyralis surmised, "Well, you can't yield richness from poorness." Shaking his head, he handed her the cloak of their partnership. "You go back to eating filaments and fungi, for no fine forage will strengthen *your* wings." And with that, Pyralis walked past her and headed for his next patch.

Maggie watched him leave; so perfect was his complexion that it was left unblemished.

CHAPTER NINE

THE MICA POOL

Maggie wandered through the night light. Why had she been so ready to follow Pyralis's rules, so easily seduced by promises of rich reward? Because she had been hoping to find a path to the rich food that would give her, a rather pedestrian mayfly, some value. And if she were more, she might be more certain of the more she was. Yet Pyralis told her that she wore her beliefs as protection against the real world, as a fabric that wrapped her from her own trivial future.

With these thoughts, Maggie had no hunger, and as water flows, she passed through one of the richest reaches she had ever seen—rocks full of glistening, ripe diatoms. She stopped and grazed some *gomphonema*, for she recognized its form, but somehow it had no taste; it did not satisfy. Her legs continued to carry her downstream—as if downstream would take her some place she hadn't been before.

Wandering aimlessly in her doubts and hurt, Maggie didn't know how close she was to becoming fish food. A sleek, silvery fish stalked her; he glided along with the current, making his wave indistinguishable from it. He tracked

Maggie downstream, waiting for the right moment to dart cross-stream to grab her.

Maggie, oblivious to where her meandering was about to take her, stepped on the antenna of a dozing crayfish. The crayfish, quite startled at being so rudely awakened, propelled himself backward at great speed and collided with the fish. The fish, hit so unexpectedly by so aggressive a foe, swam away with his life; the crayfish, being attacked from fore and aft, darted for cover; and Maggie, seeing a blur of rapid movement, froze amidst a wave of commotion. Once the waters calmed, she scurried under a rock. There, she realized what had happened. She was horrified. But then she thought of her escape—that she had escaped—and she began to laugh. She laughed until she had to stop to catch her breath, and, at that moment, she noticed a lean cluster of oval *amphoras* before her.

Amphoras were not Maggie's favorite, but she emerged from under the rock. With her eyes watching the waters above her, Maggie ate every single diatom. She had difficulty squeezing the diatoms' silica sheaths, as if from her lack of eating her mandibles had somehow weakened. Still, the *amphoras* tasted surprisingly sweet, and Maggie found herself content and full on the small bit of forage.

Laughing at herself again, Maggie headed downstream. According to Pyralis's rules, her deficit was now so large she might never catch up. Yet what had appeared to be a deficit had actually been a phantom of her own blindness. There were no rules to define what and where she should eat. That a plump, golden diatom is a rich morsel is meaningless if there is no hunger, whereas a tough, green strand can be a jewel if one is in need. She had been so busy trying to find some rules by which to assess her forage that she had missed seeing that the richness she could glean from the stream depended on how she came upon it. In all patches there was something to relish; each patch was a mosaic of possibilities through which she could take a direct path or linger. Pyralis's course might yield more weight, but to see her forage as units of yield, she risked losing the nourishment of its uniqueness. Seeking such sustenance might not be efficient, but that nourishment held the richness Maggie sought for her eggs.

Now aware of her surroundings, Maggie enjoyed the fullness of the flow that ruffled her gills and splayed her tail filaments. Traversing a dark gray plateau, she saw that although her travels had been downstream, she really had been meandering in a circle, always getting closer to the patch she sought. Perhaps her patch existed somewhere in its entirety but was rarely encountered. Or perhaps the patch she sought could not be seen, for although its ingredients lay throughout the stream, until they merged into a completed form, the patch remained an intangible entity.

Maggie stopped beside a dense *batrachospermum* bush. Its slim olive-green branches rose in whorls from thicker central stems; as a whole the bush had a violet luster. Maggie was in a stretch of stream very different from any she had seen before. The large, charcoal rocks over which she had been walking had melded to form one continuous surface. There were gullies and ridges, but the streambed was an unbroken expanse: it made the stream seem one large pool.

Maggie's attention was drawn downstream to where the gully she stood in appeared to taper. Within a narrow chasm, waters sparkled like the light of the other world; waters that were now touching Maggie's skin glowed golden. She must see this place. She hurried along the shallow gully. The current flowed fast over the rock's continuity, buoying Maggie forward but not carrying her away.

The ground rose gently into two hills, and the gap between them formed the narrow opening Maggie had seen. The waters rushed through this pass, so Maggie grasped the ground firmly and proceeded slowly. Within a short distance the pass widened, and Maggie stepped onto a ledge overlooking an enclosed valley. Before her, a basin with walls of mica glittered golden. And in this canyon, with the most delicate of bodies, was another mayfly. Rays of light seemed to radiate from this mayfly, as if her body were translucent.

The mayfly was moving forward, stepping from side to side. Maggie watched, transfixed. When the mayfly stopped her stepping, she undulated her gills, from thorax to tail, in one continuous wave that ascended smoothly and then reflected sharply when the apices of her gills reached their zenith. As her gills returned to her sides, she was buoyed off the substrate, and then, upon landing, she arched her body, stretching her head toward her tail. Then she started to step from side to side again. Maggie was amazed to see the slender mayfly prancing about in the lighted openness as she was.

When Maggie stepped into the mica pool, the other mayfly froze. Maggie quickly flurried her gills and took another step forward so that she could be clearly seen. The mayfly tilted her head graciously and came to the edge of the basin to meet Maggie.

Long, flowing, lanceolate gills fell gently at the mayfly's sides. She was wider than Maggie but flatter, and with shorter legs, she rested closer to the ground. Her skin was a soft brown mixed with yellow, and she had a very round face on a very flat head. Her smile revealed long palps covered with long bristles.

"Hello," the mayfly greeted Maggie. "I am Ephemerella."

"Hello," Maggie replied, "I'm Maggie." Then looking admiringly into the glittering basin she said, "This is a wonderful pool. Have you been here long?"

"Several night lights—I like the radiance so much." Ephemerella turned so that she could look into the pool too.

"Aren't you afraid of the openness, though?" Maggie asked.

Ephemerella shrugged her small wing pads. "Perhaps the openness does make me vulnerable, but it is here, in this openness, that I can feel the rhythm of the stream."

"How's the food?" Maggie couldn't help but ask.

"There's forage here, but I've had to roam some for variety."

"What meanderings I've been making in search of forage," Maggie conceded, laughing at herself.

"Well, apparently you've been feeding well," Ephemerella noted, looking at Maggie and grinning. Again her long palps protruded. "You're quite robust."

"Yes, all my wandering, my wondering, my looking now seems rather silly," Maggie said, venturing a few steps into the openness of the basin. "Likely I could have remained in one place and nourished just as well."

"Don't chide yourself for your travels," Ephemerella said sympathetically as she followed Maggie; "we mayflies are vagile by nature. Unable to sit and wait, we prefer to search the stream for our nourishment." She reclined on her forelegs; her tail raised into the current. "Perhaps we fear that in foraging the same reach over and over our paths will become inflexible, bringing us to nothing new. And perhaps it is in finding the novel that we learn to savor our forage."

"Seeing this canyon, though," Maggie said wistfully as she looked at the walls that rose around her, "it now seems that what I've really been looking for is a place like it, a solid rock from which I wouldn't be so readily washed away." Then looking from the walls to the light dancing in the waters, she asked the other mayfly, "In a world that is constantly changing, is there any fault with wanting a place that is always there, a place where one can trust oneself to rest?" Then mimicking Trichop, her abdomen even twitching slightly from side to side, Maggie rejoined softly, "But nothing is always there for certain, for certain."

Ephemerella, her long, pointed gills streaming beside her, glided through the waters to the wall that was glittering before Maggie. She rested her claw on it. "These walls are solid, but the waters of the stream can still carry us," she reminded Maggie. "We secure ourselves with our claws, which can grasp the ground anew, and with our ability to find sustenance in every pool. The entire reach of the stream provides us a home in which we can rest," she said softly but reassuringly; "there is no more solid ground than it. But our home in the stream is not a constant place."

In the deep, steady flow that rolled into the lighted basin Maggie recalled: "There was a pool I was washed from so many night lights ago. There, I knew the waters well and thought the entire stream would become as well known to me. I was secure that my path would determine what was on my horizon." She ventilated her gills to inhale deeply, even though the waters were rich with air. "Now it seems as if I've been standing on a rock inside myself," she tried to explain, "a rock I've secured from the currents. This rock has allowed me to retain some footing, to hold a path to a place where I might again find my grounding. But without a solid rock to stand on, each meeting seems to redefine who I am, and I become less of what I thought I was."

Ephemerella swam to her. "How fragile can be the world that gives us context," she said of the delicacy of their circumstance, "relationships woven into a fabric that gives us our meaning and home. Made of threads easily undone by change, by neglect, our context is vulnerable to even the gentlest of currents."

Maggie looked at Ephemerella, whose skin yielded to the light, allowing its rays to pass through. Then she looked at her own skin, which reflected the light back into the sparkling waters above. "How are we to find mooring in something so vulnerable?" she asked.

"We all are moored to the stream by a network of relationships, a network that intertwines transient entities with the changing substrates of the stream," Ephemerella said. "To see our context as fragile is to realize that it's fragile for all of us." Just then a spiny, green *tetraedron* ball floated by. Ephemerella jumped up, grabbed the ball in her claws, and brought it down to the ground. There, she playfully let it pop from her claws, and the algae tumbled away in the current.

When the spiny ball had disappeared, Ephemerella said, "Should we abandon our fabric because its threads are vulnerable? Or should we, instead, reinforce it, give it continuity, with the threads of our ideals?"

A voice darted through the waters of the stream, into the canyon, and straight to Maggie: "Ideals are for fish food!"

Stepping back toward the solid rock behind her, Maggie said, "I've been told that ideals are for those of us whose only value is as fish food. How can one hold one's ground with conceptions that exist only in the mind?"

"We mayflies must be able to believe in qualities embodied only ephemerally," Ephemerella said. "Of course we'd like to have a constant foundation on which to stand, but we cannot lose trust in a foundation that provides no such footing. Without carrying our ideals, our bodies have no center, becoming empty shells with no emergent spirit. What value have we then? Without our spirit, we erode into bodies of selfish appetites directed on selfish paths. So unfastened from our substrate, we do dwell in a 'fish eat fish' world."

"But how do we know that such isn't the reality of the stream?" Maggie asked as she walked toward Ephemerella for an answer. "Perhaps we shield ourselves with a vision of the stream that allows us to pass through it, missing the point of what is while trying to find a place that will never be. In the stream, a retreat without a rock doesn't hold much water."

"What rock of reference does any of us stand upon?" Ephemerella asked and then sprang from the substrate and into the basin's waters. With a touch of envy Maggie watched

Ephemerella glide away. She felt herself move forward, but her claws still tightly grasped the ground. But then she pushed against the ground and leapt up into the stream's waters too. How free and light she felt! She stretched her long, thin legs behind her, flicked her abdomen, and darted past Ephemerella. Ephemerella, laughing, raced beside her.

"We look into the stream from a rock of a nature that won't unsettle our own nature," Ephemerella said. "Securing a vantage that shields us from the current, we peer out from our fortress and gather our evidence of how the world works. But where is the boundary that delineates what we see? Qualities unseen emanate from ourselves and permeate our definitions. What we most readily perceive are the justifications for our own behavior." They made a broad left turn, skimmed the golden valley wall, and then headed groundward. "Our evidence is sculpted by the shape of the retreats we have built."

Maggie still wondered. "Can't we look into the stream and eventually all see the same thing?"

"There are rocks, food, and water," Ephemerella said, pointing to each, "water that surrounds us, permeates us, and nourishes us. Yes, there is everything to be gleaned from the stream. But will we all ever see the same thing?" Ephemerella stretched her eyes up a wall of the canyon. "I don't know," she answered and then returned her eyes to Maggie. "To tell the order from the arrangement, the process from the order, the reason from the process—we all want to know."

Ephemerella walked away from the wall and toward the center of the basin. Passing a spray of *achnanthes*, she stopped and pulled them up by their stalks. She offered the bouquet to Maggie, who politely declined it, and then she continued on her way, eating the *achnanthes*. Maggie followed her.

From the entrance to the valley, waters ran down a long slope to the deepest part of the canyon. There, the waters took one of two paths: most continued downstream, but some joined a current that rose up and then fell backward, traveled forward with new waters down the slope, and then rose in the upward sweep again. Ephemerella stopped just outside this jet of water. Maggie joined her, and with their legs folded beneath them, they sat and watched tidbits caught in the current: plants and pebbles that flowed on and those that circled round and round until they eventually escaped.

"From the stream comes to us a confusing array of information," Ephemerella said after a while. "We all just want to find a way of safe passage. In this our paths are not so different. But the rightness of each path—that truth lies somewhere beyond. We get closer, but I don't think we ever quite touch that point of knowing."

"As the point I meander around," Maggie discerned, "that point where belief is birthed into reality. But I've been told the materials for that reality don't exist, that there's nothing of the stream with which to realize my possibility and everything of our insective nature to take it apart." She looked down at the ground and examined how the small pieces of mica permeated the rock.

"To see that it's in our nature to have limits doesn't preclude that it's also in our nature to shape what is," Ephemerella said. "How do we say where it is and isn't in our nature to go? When we look at the terrain around us, of course we see evidence of the rightness of the course we've been upon: the groundwork has already been laid. But should we follow signposts that guide us to continue along paths that lead us to perpetuate poor behavior?" Ephemerella stood up. "Somewhere we are making choices; we are deciding how we should be, what of our nature we want to nurture. If we decide our direction by discerning the paths we've already taken and calling them laws, then the premise of those routes remain embedded. But instead," she faced Maggie, "can't we shape the way we live in the world, pattern a fabric not of our limits but of our visions? To look for affirmation only from where we already stand, we may miss the point of passage, and the infancy of the ideal will never grow."

Maggie looked at this tender mayfly who had traveled through the same stream as she and had arrived at this reflecting pool confident in their ephemerid vision.

"You and I look from the same rock," Maggie said, "but there is not one voice. ..."

"You can speak only your own voice," Ephemerella replied. Her gills waved in the current. "Our bodies here and gone so quickly, we mayflies hold on to qualities of like nature. Yet although we experience them ephemerally, their being is always. The times we touch their essence, we become intoxicated; to experience them is our reward. Embodied by our vision, our ideals are not depleted, but, like us, they are easily washed away if not maintained by the replenishment of our belief. We are home for and find home in these ideals, which are here, gone, but always. Don't let that vision be lost." Ephemerella let the current lift her from the substrate and carry her a few steps downstream.

Standing amid the valley's openness, Maggie listened to the irregular but constant, surrounding but sourceless voice of the stream. All around her the waters glimmered with light that appeared and disappeared, traveling along paths that never seemed repeated. Maggie brought her face to the wall of the basin. The wall glistened, each aspect sending forth a ray of light reflecting its own orientation. Yet when Maggie tried to follow one glistening path back to its origin, its luster was lost from her sight, for its radiance was created upon merging with other rays. Here, every entity, even those passing through the valley for only a moment, became party to the dance of light. Maggie looked at the light on Ephemerella's skin, continuously altering the surface seen. This basin didn't provide its travelers with simple definitions of objects. In other reaches of the stream, Maggie might step back, for distance seemed to sharpen the boundaries of an image. But now she began to wonder if distance resolved boundaries or created them.

In this wash, Maggie realized that her hunger was gone. Actually, she was feeling strange. Her skin itched her, and muscles she had never felt before were stretching and flexing. And here, in this mica canyon of solid rock, where the light of the other world danced in the stream's waters, where the other world and the stream seemed to find a way to be one, she was taken with an irresistible urge to touch the border of the two worlds. She told her companion this.

Ephemerella laughed. "It's your time."

Her time! Her time for wings—her time to fly through denselessness—her time to lay the eggs for which she had been feeding. She felt her abdomen swell. She had traveled the stream on her meandering path, and she had arrived, robust. "What should I do?" she asked.

"You already know," Ephemerella said, shaking Maggie by her wing pads. Ephemerella clasped Maggie's claw and pulled her along.

Yes. Maggie needed to find a bridge to the other world.

Maggie went slowly, savoring the richness of the golden waters. Before the basin's end was the tree that she needed.

"I guess it's time to say goodbye," Maggie said.

"Yes," Ephemerella whispered.

Maggie stepped onto the wooden limb and started to climb. She was happy that she might place her eggs on the surface of the mica pool.

CHAPTER TEN

THE WORLD OF AIR

The smooth wooden bridge arched upward into the world of air. The day had come—Maggie was leaving the stream and would never be a nymph again. Beneath her rich brown nymphal skin her adult body was a pale red, the mandibles with which she had fed were gone, and her wings were waiting, fully formed.

Suddenly, deep within, Maggie felt herself cringe from the forward motion upon which she had embarked. As much as the eggs in her swollen abdomen might be ready, she was not. She was about to leave her home, to leave its surroundingness, for a world with no familiar rocks, and she was afraid she might lose sight of herself in her new skin. This new skin would be soft; she would shed what little protection thick skin had given her as a nymph.

How different integument could be: Rensaleer's so thin, Jacob's like armor, hers somewhere between. One's skin held one together as an entity in the stream; without it, one would be too amorphous to call one's self a self.

Poor thin-skinned Rensaleer so disliked the amorphous qualities that leaked in and out of defined forms. He tried to block them from his view, for they only confused the clarity of his arrangements. And Pyralis, likewise a soft skin, shielded himself from undesirable elements with an impervious interior. But the soft, refuge-less Trichop wanted to be amorphous, so that he wouldn't recognize himself as a self and could float along, without destination, undetected. After riding the stream's currents, would he emerge with his skin calloused? In the other world, Trichop would be a fly-by-night; Pyralis's bright sunlit scales would gloss over any vulnerabilities in his exterior; and Rensaleer would emerge with his skin slightly hardened. But Maggie worried for Rensaleer, for he, having never nourished well, would be a small fly.

Like Maggie's, Rudy's integument would become softer upon emergence. Yet he wanted to replace his hard nymphal skin with one even more enduring, so that in the other world, as soft skins, he and his clan would not lose their definition.

And Loveta? Maggie peered over the edge of the bridge and looked into the waters below her. Loveta's skin never changed; it was always taut, except for the few moments just after it cleaved to vent a larger Loveta.

In a hard, adult shell Jacob's soft, larval self yearned to shed the skin that made him impermeable. But Jacob had learned that the softness hurt less when kept quiescent within, experiencing both worlds through words.

Soft skins, hard skins, they shared the stream's waters, connected by imperceptible elements that passed through them all. Maggie thought of Teresa, who would never emerge into the world of air, whose inner cavities were filled by the waters that surrounded her, whose self was only a few porous layers thick. A cool current rose from the valley's floor, carrying the scents of the substrate to Maggie. It wasn't the staying or the wandering that brought one the richness of the stream but one's permeability.

Hard skins, soft skins, we all are vulnerable streamlings, Maggie thought. But to protect against our fears, must we make ourselves impervious? Would we be undone by our connectedness? The cool waters spiraled past the tall, glittering walls of the basin and lifted Maggie's gills from her sides.

Yes, there is something we need always to protect—the spirit behind our words, the sincerity with which we speak them. But more than some outer covering we need something within that holds us intact, a quality real though immaterial, as important to the stream as are the rocks, algae, and water: a nonintegumented integrity.

And then, as quickly as it had come, Maggie's fear was gone. She knew she would recognize herself in the other world, for only an immature mayfly would yield an adult one. And if her skin were to become thinner, perhaps so much easier the breathing.

Maggie recommenced her walk along the limb. She could see the other world above her. It was a color she didn't know: a rich, dazzling brightness amid which wisps of white floated gracefully.

Maggie reached. The tip of her claw touched the boundary, the place where the stream became the other world. Yet instead of it being something she could feel, a border between the stream and denselessness, current and wind, becoming and being, it was everything of each. She brought her face to touch it.

What is this place, Jacob, what is its name? It doesn't have a face, nor can we hold it, yet without its existence we couldn't breathe. It is here that water mixes with air, the nymph with the adult, the being with the belief. Without this intermingling the boundary would be a barrier, denying passage to elements that must exist in both worlds if we are to know them in either.

Maggie passed her front legs through the boundary and into the dryness of air. Her antennae followed and then her head. She passed through the most permeable of integuments, a change of states in one entity. She was dizzied by the lightness of movement and color. A breeze, the almost imperceptible current she had felt when last at the boundary, made her face tingle.

From the stream Maggie emerged into the other world. How clumsy she felt, being pulled back by gills she would no longer need. Here the air would permeate her skin.

Stupendous trees surrounded her—enormous, deep brown trunks with broad, deep green leaves. The leaves floated in the bodiless current of the limitless sky. She heard the waters coursing below her, and someone's singing filled the air.

If there was any boundary through which Maggie had passed, it was that between her time of foraging and her time of nourishing. This was her emergence. It was her time to speak her voice, to affirm her vision. The ideal she had sought, that had filled her with hope at its possibility, that had guided her path—it was not to be shed as her nymphal skin but taken with her into adulthood.

Within moments, the skin of her larval self began to split, first across the top of her head and then down the back of her thorax. She flexed her muscles and then pulled gently. Translucent wings stretched upward and came to rest when their tips touched softly high above her back. Maggie stepped out of her nymphal skin, grasped the limb with her claws, and pulled her tail from its old encasing.

Not yet ready to fly, her reddish body still covered by a fine sheath she had yet to shed, Maggie waited to take her flight on thin, yellow-veined wings. She looked into the largeness of the world around her. Brightness surrounded the greenness that surrounded her, and the stream cleared a path through the lushness. Above the stream's surface she could see mayflies who had emerged before her, taking their first flight, testing their wings.

To fly freely in the wind must be a delicate balance, Maggie thought; to remain intact yet be buoyant, to be able to release the ground yet grasp it anew. In the stream we so fear having our claws lose grasp of the ground, for we may be thrown into a current over which we have no control. But our claws must leave the ground to fly.

To be ready to fly—how is one ready? How do we know the strength of our wings without having flown? How do we recognize the ethereal in denselessness if we cannot see it in the stream? How do we find our perch anew in this world of air?

A gentle wind whirled around Maggie. She looked down into the green-brown depth that was the stream. Although the waters were clear, she couldn't see the bottom. Still, she knew that streamlings wandered there, algae grew, and water passed. How warm was the light of the other world. She stretched her legs and flexed her wings, and then she walked to the tip of her wooden perch. High above the stream, she dug her claws into the aged wood. Is there somewhere we can fly high without seeing ourselves above the stream—a place of freedom but not abandon, where one exercises control only to maintain one's own integrity and not to deny another's?

This place, no, I can't exactly define it, set down its boundaries, say what is within and what is without. It doesn't fit an equation by which it is proven; it isn't derived from a rule or a law. It is an attitude: an attitude that there is good for the self in a common good; an attitude that we are all part of the stream, the *same* stream, and none of us is above it, for even in our emergence it has given us all we are. Maggie wove the threads of her fabric. It is an attitude that the most will come to us not by taking the most but by maintaining the well-being of the stream we all inhabit, for this stream will always provide us a home, if we can realize its wholeness beyond our experience of it.

Maggie looked up into the brightness above her and tried to fathom its vastness. Pyralis would say I'm rewriting reality to make it palatable. But if we don't believe in the world we want, how will it be? Is its realization to be another time, another place—here is the world we know. Are we to wait for its perfection elsewhere—its ingredients lie throughout the stream. They are here if they are anywhere, they are now if they are any time. Our behavior in the world affects the nature of the world. We create our fabric. So we must be our best. Now. Not tomorrow but today. Not sometimes but always. Not in another world but here in our home. The boundary between the worlds of water and air is not a barrier, keeping our insectiveness within and the freedom of denselessness without.

Someone with extremely long legs flew by overhead. His long, transparent wings quickly took him out of sight. Somehow Maggie knew he was a cranefly. Green blades bent gently in the bodiless current, and the sweetest of scents filled the lightness that was air. Ribbons of pink spread amid the wisps of white that hung in the sky.

Can we elevate ourselves above our own smallness to a world in which we all emerge with our integrity intact? Can we be ethereal beings in a concrete world? Maggie asked. I look toward the emergence of a nonintegumented integrity, an entity without walls, without hierarchy, held together by a unity born of respect. It is the sharing that is vital to making a vision grow—I will cast my eggs upon the water.

A breeze washed Maggie's body, pressing against her wings and tickling her tail.

"What a silly mayfly I am to be saying such things," she whispered from her perch. The thin sheath that had been covering Maggie's body now peeled away, revealing below a skin shiny and bright. Her delicate wings glistened in the sun, hinted at by only the veins that held them together. She would take her flight on these thin wings, whose strength was not in resisting the denselessness but riding it, riding those qualities whose intangible nature would make Maggie buoyant. These wings she would have only for a day—to take her through denselessness—to take her to make more of her kind—more ephemerids—to take her to fill the world with fish food.

"Fish food!" Maggie stretched her wings out to her sides and brought them back above her. "Yes! Fish food!" She stretched her wings out again and this time brought them down. "Whose ideals keep them moving until their day comes!" Her claws left the ground.

Maggie flew into a delicate mass of mayflies, a mass with no center, for it is the strength of the whole that keeps an ethereal body airborne. Maggie flew into a cloud of her kind, an ephemeral cloud, one that was there and then would be gone but would return another tomorrow.

THE END

ACKNOWLEDGMENTS

The story behind this novel is germane to these acknowledgments. My interest in freshwater ecology began as an undergraduate. As I pursued my Master's degree, studying stream-dwelling insects, I found myself as interested in the scientists around me as the science, perhaps more so. I would like to acknowledge my professors in the field of aquatic ecology, Drs. Alan Baker, James Haney, and Sam Mozley, and also David Lenat, who shared his practical knowledge of the field and enthusiasm for it. And I would like to thank those scientists, who shall remain unnamed, who inspired the characters herein.

This novel was drafted many years ago, so I may forget to thank some of those who along the way have read it and offered comments. With that caveat, I would like to thank Pamela Hundt Reid, Karen Kester, Michael P. King, Taina Litwak, Karen McCarthy Eger, Charles Mitter, Linda Mussehl, Jim Ott, Leland Ott, Amy Scheck, Debby Silverfine, Pearl Silverfine, and Jil Swearingen. Betty Abolafia Rosensweig, Laura Mansberg Cotterman, and Beth Dawson Staehle also offered support in this endeavor.

And to John Cowgell, Taina Litwak, Charles Mitter, and Jim Ott, I thank you for your support along the way and encouragement to bring this work to fruition. Finally, I would like to thank Black Rose Writing for publishing this quirky novel.

ABOUT THE AUTHOR

From living above her parents' hardware store in Brooklyn to living a mile down a gravel road in semi-rural Texas with her husband, two sons, and the local wildlife, Eva Silverfine has explored a variety of urban to rural landscapes. On that journey, she earned two degrees in the environmental sciences, worked in a research lab, and eventually retooled as a copyeditor. She freelances for several academic presses and writes personal narrative and fiction in the in-between spaces. Her short fiction has appeared in a variety of journals; she has published a collection of essays, *Elastic Walls*; and her debut novel, *How to Bury Your Dog*, was published by Black Rose Writing in 2021.

NOTE FROM THE AUTHOR

Word-of-mouth is crucial for any author to succeed. If you enjoyed *Ephemeral Wings*, please leave a review online—anywhere you are able. Even if it's just a sentence or two. It would make all the difference and would be very much appreciated.

Thanks!
Eva Silverfine

We hope you enjoyed reading this title from:

BLACK ROSE writing™

www.blackrosewriting.com

Subscribe to our mailing list—*The Rosevine*—and receive **FREE** books, daily deals, and stay current with news about upcoming releases and our hottest authors.

Scan the QR code below to sign up.

Already a subscriber? Please accept a sincere thank you for being a fan of Black Rose Writing authors.

View other Black Rose Writing titles at www.blackrosewriting.com/books and use promo code **PRINT** to receive a **20% discount** when purchasing.